"I'm sorry...did I startle you?"

As she inconspicuously clung to the baby in fear, Alexa gazed up into cold, arctic-blue eyes that stabbed her with an intensity that left her legs weak. Did this man recognize her for the fraud that she was? To hide her fear, Alexa kept her expression haughty as she glared at him. "What do you want?" she demanded in as strong a voice as her terror-filled chest would allow.

The stony lines of his mouth and chin softened slightly as if he were amused by her autocratic behavior. "Allow me to introduce myself, Mrs. Santini. I'm Damas Silva, your new bodyguard. I'll be accompanying you on your vacation. The car is waiting. Shall we?"

Dear Reader,

What is it about mysterious men that always makes our pulse race? Whether it's the feeling of risk or the excitement of the unknown, dangerous men have always been a part of our fantasies, and now they're a part of Harlequin Intrigue. Throughout 1995, we'll kick off each month with a DANGEROUS MAN. This month, meet Damas Silva in the *Bodyguard* by Leona Karr.

A multipublished author, Leona Karr pursued a career as a reading specialist until her first suspense book was published in 1980. She lives near Boulder, Colorado, and the Rocky Mountains. When she isn't reading and writing, she happily spends her time spoiling a gaggle of giggling granddaughters.

With our DANGEROUS MAN promotion, Harlequin Intrigue promises to keep you on the edge of your seat...and the edge of desire.

Sincerely,

Debra Matteucci
Senior Editor and Editorial Coodinator
Harlequin Books
300 East 42nd Street, Sixth Floor
New York, NY 10017

Bodyguard

Leona Karr

Harlequin Books

TORONTO • NEW YORK • LONDON
AMSTERDAM • PARIS • SYDNEY • HAMBURG
STOCKHOLM • ATHENS • TOKYO • MILAN
MADRID • WARSAW • BUDAPEST • AUCKLAND

To Barbara Blackman with love—a delightful friend
who is always there for me.

ISBN 0-373-22309-9

BODYGUARD

Copyright © 1995 by Leona Karr

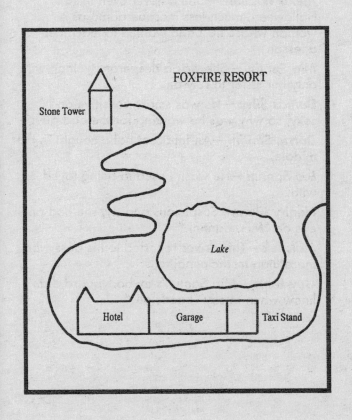

FOXFIRE RESORT

Stone Tower

Lake

Hotel   Garage   Taxi Stand

CAST OF CHARACTERS

Alexa Widmire—She'd never even liked Halloween, much less masquerading as a woman whose husband wanted to teach her a lesson.

Mia Santini—She was a desperate woman with only her sister to rely on.

Damas Silva—He was smart, sensitive and sexy, so why was he working for the bad guys?

Dorrie Santini—An innocent babe caught in the middle.

Leo Santini—He wasn't used to being toyed with.

Nanny Clara—Suspicious and sly, she had an eye on "Mrs. Santini."

Malchek—This driver reported to his boss—on more than traffic conditions.

Guy Lentz—Mia Santini's ex-bodyguard didn't know when to say "hands off."

Chapter One

Alexa Widmire turned off the water, stepped out of the shower and swore as the doorbell rang again. She had delayed her shower until midmorning in order to enjoy a leisurely beginning to her three-week hiatus from teaching American history at Hunter College. She grabbed a terry-cloth bathrobe and pattered barefoot through the small apartment.

The doorbell rang again with a frantic insistence. Alexa brushed a strand of wet blond hair from her face and squinted through the peephole. Then she quickly unlocked the door. "Mia, what a surprise!"

Her sister limped into the room. Her usually carefully styled hair was a disheveled tangle on her shoulders, the collar on a pink silk blouse lay turned under and her short white linen skirt was twisted to one side. She grabbed Alexa's arm. "You've got to help me." And she began to cry hysterically.

"What's the matter? What's happened?" Alexa helped her to the sofa. "Have you been in an accident?"

"No, I...I..." Tears spilled down Mia's cheeks and she put a hand up to her trembling lips. "I'm so frightened," she sobbed. "You'll help me, won't you? Oh, please, Alexa, please."

"Of course," Alexa soothed, sitting down beside her sister and putting an arm around her trembling shoulders. She couldn't imagine what had sent Mia into such a state. Her sister was still somewhat of a stranger to her because the two of them had just recently found each other. Left at an orphanage as infants, the identical twin girls had been adopted by different families—Alexa by a couple who were university professors, while Mia was raised as the daughter of a powerful Sicilian family. The two young women, now in their late twenties, had made contact with each other through Alexa's efforts to locate her birth mother. The discovery that she had a twin sister had made up for the disappointment of learning that their natural mother was deceased.

"I don't know what to do," Mia said, still sobbing. "It's…Guy. They took him away. You've got to help me. My husband mustn't find out."

"Find out what?" Alexa's stomach took a sickening plunge. She'd never met Leo Santini, but she'd seen his picture in the paper—a bullish physique, heavy facial features and masses of curly iron gray hair. The feds had been trying to collect enough evidence to bring him to court for illegal enterprises. Mia had not told her husband about the sisters finding each other a few months earlier. "He likes to control everything and everybody," Mia had explained. "Leo would make sure that we never saw each other." The helplessness in her sister's eyes had told Alexa a lot about the man that Mia had married.

"I'm so frightened," she repeated. She gripped Alexa's hand tightly. "Leo mustn't know that I was there . . . in Guy's apartment, when his men took him away." Her voice shook.

"I don't understand," said Alexa but she was afraid she did. Her mouth was suddenly dry. "What happened?"

Mia shuddered. "We heard this pounding on the door. And men's voices. I grabbed my things, fled into the bathroom and locked the door. Guy let them in. I heard furniture knocked over, a lot of shouting and fighting." She took a shaky breath. "They took him away. I don't know if Leo found out about us—"

"Who's Guy?"

Mia's moist eyes took on a soft glint. "An ex-football player. Lovely brown eyes and sandy hair. He was kicked out of the National League a year ago for betting. Leo was mixed up in the illegal scheme, so when the whole mess blew up, he gave Guy a job as my bodyguard."

Alexa didn't need much imagination to know where Mia's story was going. A lonely wife and an attractive man in constant close contact—trouble!

"I don't know what I can do—" Alexa began.

Mia didn't let her finish. "I need you to run an errand for me," she said with a rush. "I don't think anyone knew I was in the apartment . . . but I'm not sure. Guy's been gambling and losing a lot lately—owes the syndicate a lot of money. Maybe that's why Leo's men took him away. I can't be sure. If he knows about Guy and me . . ." She put both hands over her face. Her body shook with sobs again.

Alexa went into the bathroom for a glass of water and a couple of aspirin. "How long has this been going on?" Alexa asked after her sister had swallowed the pills.

Mia took a deep breath. "A couple of months. It just happened. Leo's been away a lot. We started stopping off at Guy's apartment..." Her voice trailed off.

"And you're sure no one saw you there this morning?"

"I don't know. His apartment is at the back of a converted old mansion. We always come and go from the alley. I turned my ankle on the back stairs when I rushed out." Tears welled in her eyes. "You've got to help me. There's no one else."

"But what can I—"

"My earrings." Mia pulled at her earlobes. "I left them on the bed stand. Leo gave them to me...my initials in diamonds. If someone finds them there..." Her voice rose hysterically. "You don't know Leo. He's cruel and heartless. He knows how much I love my baby." Her panic-stricken eyes sought Alexa's. "I'll never see Dorrie again if he follows through with his threats to send her away. He'll take her from me— I know he will." Mia crumpled into a sobbing heap.

Alexa was completely at a loss. Her staid life as a college professor was well ordered and comfortably dull. Her romantic encounters with eligible men had been as sensible as everything else in her life. She'd never experienced any wild senseless passion. She couldn't imagine herself getting embroiled in the kind of emotional upheaval that Mia had brought upon herself. Alexa swallowed the impulse to lecture her sister. This wasn't the time to point out that Mia had been a fool to cheat on her husband.

"Leo will kill me if he finds out. He's made arrangements for me to leave for an upstate resort this afternoon. He'll join me there in a few days. Now... now I don't know what to do," she cried hysterically. My ankle..." She grimaced as she eased a swollen foot out of her white sling pump. "I can't walk. You have to do this for me. Please... please, Alexa. Go back to the apartment for me. Get my earrings before somebody else finds them."

The request was so unexpected and bizarre that Alexa couldn't find the words to respond. Her overriding common sense told her to say emphatically, "No, I don't want to get involved," but she hesitated. Her newly found relationship with Mia promised the kind of closeness and joy that she'd always longed for. Raised as an only child by older adoptive parents, she had felt that she didn't really belong to anyone. Looking into her sister's pleading face, Alexa knew that the strength of her longed-for family tie was being put to the test. This was her blood sister asking for help. If she turned her back on her, the bond between them would surely be broken forever.

Mia's wails rose. "Leo swears that I'll never see my baby daughter again if he decides to toss me aside. He'll take her away from me forever."

"No, he won't. He can't do that. The law won't let him."

Mia gave a crazy, tearful laugh. "And what does the law have to do with Leo Santini? He gets his way no matter what."

Alexa was well aware of Mia's husband's power. The newspapers were full of Santini's questionable dealings, but despite all the efforts of law-enforcement agencies to find solid evidence against him, they had come up empty-handed.

"Please help me," Mia begged. "There's no one else I can turn to," she reiterated.

Alexa silently called herself an utter fool. "All right. I'll go get the earrings."

"Thank you . . . thank you," Mia whimpered.

"Lie back on the couch and put your ankle up. As soon as I get back, we'll decide what to do next."

"I don't know what I'd do without you," Mia sobbed. "I don't have the strength to stand up to Leo anymore." She was on the edge of collapse.

Her sister had probably been emotionally abused her whole marriage, thought Alexa. Anger fueled her movements as she quickly dressed in a pair of blue jeans and a sleeveless blue striped blouse. She dried her honey blond hair, which was the same shade as her twin sister's. They both wore their hair shoulder length, but Mia liked hers in loose curls around her face, whereas Alexa pulled hers back into a casual twist, which she had decided was more dignified for a college professor.

Mia's face was slightly more rounded, but their features were identical—dusky blue eyes, noses with a slight, saucy upturn, nicely curved mouths with a matching dimple in the right cheek. Mia's behavior was consistent with her upbringing—emotional, out-going and mercurial—while Alexa was quietly in control, and certainly not given to mad impulses. She couldn't believe that she had agreed to get involved in Mia's sordid affair.

ALEXA'S HANDS were moist with nervous sweat as she clenched the steering wheel of her secondhand Chevy coupe and drove to the address Mia had given her. She'd heard enough ugly stories about mob leaders to be scared. She prayed she could get in and out of Guy's apartment without being seen. What would she say if someone stopped her? Where had Santini's men taken Guy? What if the police came looking for him? What if— *Stop it!* No use letting anxiety foster a lot of "what ifs."

She reached the address and found a large stone mansion that had obviously been a single dwelling in its grander days. The land around it had been sold for other developments and the big house's many rooms had been chopped up into utility apartments. Mia had said that Guy's place was on the ground floor at the back of the house and that there was space to park in the alley. Alexa didn't see anyone as she got out of the car behind the house.

Fingering the key that Mia had given her, she hastily walked past a wooden fence edging the property until she came to a sagging gate standing half-open beside a brimming trash bin. The backyard of the house was desolate, with old trees and scraggly shrubs the only vegetation left of what might have been a formal garden at one time.

As she hurried down a crumbling, narrow sidewalk, three stories of windows looked down at her with bleak, opaque eyes. She could feel her skin prickling as she mounted three warped steps and inserted a key in the lock. She turned the knob and pushed the door open.

An ominous silence greeted her.

Her heartbeat raced as she quickly closed the door behind her and leaned back against it, surveying the small kitchen and listening for sounds from the rest of the apartment.

Dirty dishes filled the sink. Beer cans and refuse overflowed the garbage can. A rancid smell of something decaying mingled with a closed, fusty odor. Mia's bodyguard hadn't spent much time on housekeeping chores, thought Alexa with a distasteful quiver of her nose. Why had her sister allowed herself to become entangled with such a man?

Find the earrings and get out of here. Her footsteps sounded loudly on the worn linoleum as she crossed the kitchen to a doorway leading into a small living room. She caught her breath. The place was a mess— but not from lazy housekeeping. A chair and coffee table had been turned over and a lamp lay in shattered pieces in the middle of the floor.

Mia had been right. There had been a fight. Guy had not gone willingly. The knowledge filled Alexa with new urgency. She had to find Mia's earrings and get away from the place as quickly as possible.

Gingerly she stepped around the overturned furniture and hurried down a short hall leading to a bathroom and small bedroom. She hesitated in the bedroom doorway. Brown plaid drapes flanked two windows and muted light came through a glass door opening onto a small screened porch that was cluttered with stacked boxes. Alexa wavered about turning on the light, even though the only view beyond the small porch was more of the sagging wooden fence.

As she traversed the room, she was painfully aware of the rumpled bed and the faint scent of Mia's perfume. A silk scarf dangled over the arm of one chair and Alexa grabbed it. Mia must have missed it in her haste to dress and leave the apartment.

What else had she forgotten?

Mia said she'd left her earrings on the nightstand and Alexa caught sight of a reassuring glint beside a small lamp. She reached for the earrings and a jolt of panic went through her. The cluster of diamonds belonged to *one* earring. Where was the other one?

She moved the bed lamp, pushed aside cigarette butts in an overflowing ash tray and picked up an empty glass that smelled strongly of wine. No earring. Her heart began to thump. *It had to be there.*

She went down on her knees. Anxiously she peered beneath the nightstand. Nothing but a couple of more cigarette butts. She poked her head under the bed— and let out a sigh of relief. A sparkle winked back at her. A spurt of relief made her weak. In her haste Mia must have knocked the earring on the floor and sent it sailing to rest against the foot of the bed.

Alexa took a deep breath to still her speeding pulse. Her well-ordered life-style had not prepared her for such Hollywood dramatics. A self-mocking laugh rose in her throat. She mentally chided herself for giving in to a case of nerves. Her moment of relief lasted only a split second. Before she could move to the foot of the bed to retrieve the earring, her ears caught the muffled sound of the front door opening and closing.

She froze. Her heart stopped as heavy footsteps crossed the living room and went into the kitchen.

Someone was in the apartment.

Had Guy come back? Was it safe to show herself and explain why she was cowering in his bedroom? But what if it wasn't him? What if it was one of Leo Santini's men? Had he sent someone to search for evidence that Mia and Guy had been lovers? The terror she had seen on her sister's face warned her that the situation could turn ugly very fast. How could she explain her presence in the apartment without involving her sister?

Her mind raced. She couldn't get away out the back door...not with the unknown person in the kitchen. The front door? Yes, maybe she could get out of the apartment that way. The door was out of view of the kitchen. If she was fast enough she could make it out before the person came back into the living room.

With her ear cocked to catch any sound, she paused in the doorway of the bedroom. She took two steps down the hall and then heard the person leave the kitchen and come into the living room.

She spun on her heels, dashed back into the bedroom and frantically looked for someplace to hide. A closet door stood half-open, but it was crammed so full of clothes that even a person as slender as she was couldn't have squeezed into it. If she crawled under the bed she wouldn't have a chance to bolt if she was discovered. Nothing else in the bedroom offered any hope of concealment.

Alexa quickly moved across the bedroom to the glass door between the two windows. A skeleton key dangled in the lock. She gave it a turn with her trembling fingers and pulled on the tarnished brass knob. The door opened with a loud creak. She quickly went out and closed it behind her. She saw then that the screened-in area wasn't a porch at all, just an enclosure. No exit. She was trapped. She dived behind one of the stacks of cardboard boxes, praying that she'd been quick enough not to be seen from inside the bedroom.

She cowered there, unable to hear anything except the pounding of her heart and the sound of a dog barking a few yards away. For an agonizing eternity she waited, ready to move if she heard the creak of the door opening. Every sensory bud in her body threatened to explode. Was the person still in the apartment? In the bedroom? Was he looking out the glass door that very minute? Was it possible that whoever it was might have left the apartment without coming into the bedroom?

Her ears strained to hear any sound coming from inside the apartment. Nothing. As the moments passed, the hope that the person had left grew. If the apartment was empty again, she could get the earring as planned and be gone without anyone knowing she'd been there.

She peeked around the tumbled boxes. A man stood just inside the door with his back to her. Black hair brushed the collar of his tan tweed jacket. He turned his head and his profile was not reassuring. A bold forehead and a strong nose and chin matched the hard set of his mouth.

Alexa ducked back and put a closed fist over to her mouth to muffle her breathing. It wasn't Guy. He had sandy hair. One of Santini's men must have come back. *Leo will kill me.* Her sister's sobs echoed in her ears.

If only I'd been quicker, agonized Alexa. *If only—Stop it,* she ordered. Considering the precarious situation, she had done the best she could. She had removed the scarf and one earring. The other one was out of sight, and since the man wasn't Guy, chances were that he wouldn't stay long in the apartment.

Minutes crept by. Her back and legs began to ache from their cramped position. Dust from the clutter floated up into her nostrils and she fought back a tormenting urge to sneeze. She finally decided to gamble that the man had gone. She eased out from behind the boxes, scurried to the side of one of the windows and pressed herself up against the wall. After a long moment she dared a furtive look into the bedroom. No sign of the man in the tweed jacket. The room appeared just as it had earlier. He must have gone or was in another room of the apartment. She had no choice but to take a chance and go back in the bedroom.

Her mouth dry and every muscle tensed, she eased the door opened and slipped back into the bedroom. A hushed, empty silence greeted her. No sound of movement or footsteps anywhere in the apartment. She let out the breath she had been holding. Quickly she bent down and ducked her head to locate the earring resting at the foot of the bed.

She stared with disbelief. The earring was gone.

Chapter Two

She couldn't believe it! *The man had found the earring.* Rising panic sent a tremor through her body as she stood up. Who was he? What did it mean? *I have to get out of here.* The evidence that Mia had been in the apartment was in someone else's hands. There was nothing she could do now but get away before the man or someone else stopped her.

She peered down the short hall, listening for any sound that she wasn't alone. Pressing against the hall wall, she moved slowly and cautiously. She couldn't hear anything but her own muffled breathing. Cold sweat beaded on her forehead. She probably would have fainted dead away if she'd run into anyone face-to-face.

The front door was closed as she passed it and the living room was in the same chaotic state as before. She dodged overturned furniture, crossed the living room and peered into the kitchen. No sign that anyone had been there. Everything was the same—the rancid smells, the kitchen mess. She wouldn't have known that a man had been in the apartment moments earlier if she hadn't seen him. But he had been there. And he had taken the earring.

Alexa let herself out the back door and fled down the warped steps, almost tripping on the uneven boards the way Mia must have when she'd twisted her ankle. She hurried down the cracked, uneven sidewalk and had just reached the back gate, when a boy about ten years old came around the corner of the house. He was carrying a black plastic trash bag and was heading toward the Dumpster. She gave him a fleeting look and hurried through the back gate into the alley, where her car was parked. She heard him toss the garbage sack on top of the overflowing Dumpster. He had seen her—she was certain of that. *It doesn't matter,* she told herself. She'd not been caught inside the apartment and that was the main thing.

She quickly backed out of the parking space and drove away. Her heart raced, her stomach was queasy and she felt as weak as a wet paper towel. It took several minutes for her sensible self to assert itself. *Don't be ridiculous,* she scolded herself. Nearly being caught in Guy's apartment had thrown her for a loop, but there was no sense in getting caught up in Mia's terror. It was time to view the whole thing sensibly. She'd simply tried to do an errand for her sister and had failed. Raised by logical parents to handle problems in a calm and rational way, she would help her sister look at the situation in a critical light. Between the two of them, they could decide what Mia should do to protect herself and Dorrie.

By the time she'd returned to her apartment, Alexa's sensible nature had brought her emotions back under control. She silently upbraided herself for having put herself in such a precarious position in the first place. Mia's hysterics had clouded her judgment. Her sister was clearly tottering on the edge of a nervous breakdown and Alexa had been frightened by her twin's near emotional collapse. She desperately wanted to stand by her newly found sibling, but she was painfully aware that she knew very little about Mia or her life-style. She and Mia looked alike, had the same heredity, but environment had shaped them differently.

"I'm back," Alexa announced in a feigned cheery voice as she let herself in the apartment.

Mia was still on the sofa, her ankle swollen to twice its size. There was a pile of sodden tissues beside her and her face was ravaged with tears. She sat up quickly and winced with pain as she moved her leg. "I'm so happy you're back," she breathed. "You found the place all right? You took such a long time, I thought something had happened." There was petulant accusation in her tearful tone.

Alexa handed Mia the scarf. "Is it yours?"

"Oh, yes. I forgot all about it. I was in such a hurry. I was so scared I just grabbed up everything and ran into the bathroom. I didn't even think about checking to make sure I had everything after the men had gone."

Alexa took a deep breath. "While I was there someone came into the apartment. I didn't know what to do. I could hear him in the kitchen. I dashed out on that porch and hid behind a stack of boxes. He didn't see me."

"Did you see him?"

"I caught a glimpse through the glass door."

"Who was it?" Mia's question held a spurt of hope. "Guy? Was it Guy?"

"He didn't match your description. His hair was black, longish on his collar. Wore a tan tweed jacket."

Mia's face fell in disappointment. "I thought maybe . . . maybe Guy had come back."

"Do you have any idea who the man might have been?"

"One of Leo's thugs, probably. It's a good thing you got my earrings."

"I found this one on the bedside table." Alexa handed her the earring. "You must have knocked the other one on the floor. It was under the far end of the bed."

"You've saved my life." She took the earring and then looked at Alexa's empty hand. "Where's the other one?" Her voice rose. "You got both of them, didn't you?"

"I didn't have a chance to get the one under the bed. The man came in and I had to hide."

"But after he left?" she insisted. "Why didn't you get it after he left?"

"Because when I searched for it under the bed, it was gone."

A look of horror crossed Mia's face. "Gone? What do you mean gone?"

"The man must have taken it."

"Oh, no." All color drained from her face. "He'll give it to Leo. When he sees the earring, he'll know everything."

Alexa took her hand and squeezed it. "I'm sorry...I really am. I don't know what more we can do. We'll just have to wait and see what happens."

Mia fell silent. She nervously bit on her lower lip and stared for a long time at some unseen point beyond Alexa. Then she turned and said in a choked voice, "There still may be time."

Alexa stiffened. She could tell from her sister's changing expression that her mind was whirling at a furious pace. "Time for what?"

"Don't you see?" Sudden hope shone in Mia's moist eyes. "You could go get the baby and bring her back here."

"What?" Alexa was certain she had misunderstood.

"Pick up Dorrie. Bring her back here."

"You're out of your mind, Mia. Nobody's going to let me waltz off with your baby. I've already been guilty of breaking and entering. I'm not setting myself up for a kidnapping charge."

"Just listen. Please, please listen." She clutched Alexa's hand with vicelike fingers. "It would be easy. If we move quickly, we'll have the baby out of the house before Leo knows what's happening. Then he can carry out his threat to divorce me. I won't care. I'll have Dorrie."

Alexa couldn't believe what she was hearing. "Mia, it wouldn't work."

"Yes, it would," she insisted stubbornly. "I can't walk on my ankle or I'd go myself. You have to go for me. It'll be easy. You just go into the house, get the baby and walk out."

"And if someone should see me? They'd call the police and—"

"Not if they thought you were me," Mia said smugly.

"What—?"

"With you wearing my clothes, no one would give you a second look. I haven't told anyone I have a twin sister. The baby's nanny won't object to your taking Dorrie. Clara's basically lazy and fat. Leo hired her because she's some distant relative. He surrounds himself with people who belong to the Santini family. Clara watches television most of the day in a sitting room adjoining the nursery." Mia looked at her watch. "It's another hour before the baby wakes up for her bottle. She'll be sleeping in her crib."

Alexa stared in disbelief. "I can't do it, Mia."

Mia went on as if Alexa hadn't spoken. "Just park my car in the garage. Go in the house through the side door. Get the baby, bring her back here and—"

"Absolutely not," Alexa said in her professional tone. "I can't imagine that you're serious."

Mia's unblinking eyes locked on Alexa's face. "If we don't get the baby out of the house, I could lose her forever."

"You're being overly dramatic. Leo can't keep you from your child."

"You don't know him. He takes what he wants. He has money and power—and he knows how to use both. If we don't get Dorrie out of his house now, I may never be allowed to see her again." Mia reached into her leather purse and took out a plastic folder filled with baby pictures. She handed them to Alexa. "That's Dorrie, four months."

A beautiful wide-eyed baby gazed back at Alexa from the photos. Blond hair, smoky blue eyes and an upturned nose. She had a broad, toothless grin that went straight to Alexa's heart. For a moment she couldn't think of anything but the miracle that this baby was related to her. She was family. The physical likeness was so similar Alexa could have been looking at one of her own baby pictures. Peculiar feelings stirred in her as if this beautiful little girl belonged to her in some strange, wonderful way.

Mia said quietly, "She's your niece. If Leo has his way you may never hold Dorrie in your arms or get to know her. She'll be lost to you in the same way she'll be gone to me—unless you help."

Alexa stiffened against a barrage of conflicting emotions. "I can't do it, Mia."

"Yes, you can. If we move quickly, we'll have the baby safely here with us in an hour. It's the only way. You go to my house, take her out of the nursery the same way I would and no one will give you a second look. In my clothes, with your hair the way I wear it, you can walk in and out of the house without anyone the wiser. Leo doesn't know about you . . . he won't have any idea where the baby and I have gone. That will give me time to get a lawyer and protect myself. Please, Alexa. For me . . . for Dorrie."

"And what if something goes wrong?" Alexa protested. "What if Leo comes home?"

"He won't leave his office till after lunch. That's why you've got to hurry. I'll fix your hair. You'll need more lipstick and heavier blue eye shadow." Mia began taking off her expensive peach-colored linen shirt and designer silk blouse. "Here, put on these. What size shoes do you wear?"

"Seven and a half," answered Alexa, as if this were some kind of a normal conversation."

"Good. My white pumps will fit perfectly."

"Mia, I...I can't." How could she walk into a strange house and steal a baby? She'd never taken as much as a postage stamp without permission. Going to Guy's apartment had frightened her more than anything she'd ever done—and that was only breaking and entering! What Mia proposed was kidnapping! "What if I'm caught?"

"Then we'll just have to admit the whole thing," she assured Alexa. "Don't you see? You're my sister. I sent you after my baby. It's as simple as that. You can't be charged with anything if I have given you permission to bring Dorrie to me. I'm her mother."

"Why don't I just go to your house, tell the nanny who I am and explain that you asked me to bring the baby—"

"Because she wouldn't let you take her without Leo's permission. But if she thinks you're me, there'll be no problem. As I said, no one knows I have a sister. Not even Leo. I knew he'd find out eventually about you, but I wanted to keep you to myself as long as I could. And now I'm glad—"

"There should be another way," Alexa persisted, a feeling of quicksand under her feet.

"Please, Alexa," begged Mia. "We have to try. If the plan works, Dorrie will be with me. If it doesn't, we won't have lost anything by trying."

"I don't think it's that simple." Alexa handed back the pictures of the precious baby.

"Think about it," pleaded Mia.

How could she think with Mia looking at her so hopefully? She walked over to the window and gazed down into the street below. Everything was normal—cars going by, people walking along the sidewalks, the wail of a police siren sounding on a nearby street. This morning when she drank her cup of coffee and list-lessly read the paper only an uneventful boring day lay ahead. Now her mind reeled with decisions that could affect her whole life.

How could she let some mob boss cheat her out of knowing and loving her niece? She wanted to watch the little girl grow, buy her presents and share the ex-citement of the holidays with her. No more loneliness and that horrible feeling of displacement. She would have Mia and Dorrie to fill the void that had haunted her ever since she'd learned that she was adopted. What if Mia was right? What if Santini sent the baby away and successfully removed her from her mother forever? The three of them would never get to know and love one another.

Alexa's temper suddenly flared. She hated selfish manipulating people. There wasn't a doubt in her mind that Leo Santini was as ruthless as Mia had said. She turned around and walked back to the sofa. "All right. No harm in seeing if your crazy idea works."

They hugged each other. "Thank you...thank you," bubbled Mia.

"Don't thank me yet," Alexa cautioned. It was much too early for celebrating.

Nothing lost by trying, Alexa kept repeating to her-self as she changed into Mia's clothes. Either she would be successful in taking the baby out of the house or she wouldn't. No need for that sick feeling in her stomach and hot sweat in the palms of her hands. She would be on an errand for her sister. It was as simple as that.

She brushed her hair loose on her shoulders and used a curling iron to curl her bangs and create ringlets framing her face the way Mia had.

"You need more makeup. Sit down here beside me," Mia ordered. She dived into her expensive alligator purse and took out eye shadow, lipstick, pink blush and powder. As if she were working on her own face, Mia applied the cosmetics—gray blue eye shadow to bring out the dusky tones in Alexa's eyes, bright coral lipstick to round her sensuous full lips and pink blush to highlight her cheekbones.

"There," she said with satisfaction, surveying her sister's transformation. "You'll easily pass for me."

In Mia's clothes, with her hairstyle and tasteful makeup, Alexa found the reflection in the mirror reassuring. She was her sister's image. Mia was right. They could easily pass for each other.

"The clothes are too tight," Alexa complained. She was appalled at the way the silk blouse molded her breasts and the short linen skirt cupped her fanny.

"If you have it, sister, dear, flaunt it," Mia chided. She pulled off her wedding rings and slipped them on Alexa's finger. "Here's my purse. The keys to my car are inside. When you get to the house, push the remote control on the sun visor and the gate will open. Drive into the left side of the garage. There's a passageway next to the house and a side door that leads into a long hall." She brought out a ring of keys. "This one will unlock the side door. Once inside the house, go down the hall and up the main stairs to the second floor. The nursery and nanny's quarters are to the left of the landing, at the far end of the house.

Dorrie will be taking her morning nap in her crib. Just walk into the nursery and get her."

"What if the nanny's there?"

"I told you. Clara watches soap operas almost all morning while the baby sleeps. Just call out to her that you're taking Dorrie and walk out again. I do that sometimes and she just grunts and goes back to her TV."

"Anybody else in the house?" Alexa asked, unable to believe she had committed herself to this preposterous impersonation.

"The butler's name is Archer and the housemaid is Myrna. The cook, Mrs. Delgado, never leaves the kitchen. You'll only be in the house a few minutes and shouldn't run into any of them. If you do, just avoid looking at them directly and walk away without any explanation. Act as if you belong there and no one will question what you do." She gave Alexa a quick kiss on the cheek. "Once you see Dorrie, you'll be glad that you did this for all of us. For an hour, just pretend you're me."

A feeling of rising confidence surprised Alexa. She glanced at her watch. Eleven o'clock. By noon the baby should be safe in her mother's arms. What happened after that would take some careful thought.

"You try to rest," Alexa instructed. "I'll fix us some lunch as soon as I get back. And don't worry, Mia." She gave her sister a hug. "I'll bring Dorrie safely to you."

Her sense of confidence evaporated before she'd gone two blocks from the apartment. Mia's new white BMW, with leather seats and luxurious interior mocked her for the imposter that she was. The closest she'd come to an automobile with that kind of price tag was a commercial on TV. She felt as uncomfortable in the car as she did in Mia's clothes.

By the time she had reached the elite neighborhood, with its imposing huge houses, she was ready to turn around and drive back home without even trying to carry out the impersonation. The memory of the baby's bright eyes and broad smile in the photos was the prod that kept her going.

The Santini home was set back from the street. A wide driveway led to the front of the house and to a multicar garage on the right. Alexa turned off the street and stopped in front of a wide, ornate gate. With nervous fingers she touched the remote control that was fastened to the sun visor. The gate glided open. With white-knuckled hands gripping the steering wheel, she headed up the driveway.

The garage door was open and she drove into an empty space, closest to the side of the house as Mia had instructed. She turned off the engine, and for a long moment, like someone caught in the middle of a bad dream she just sat there. *What am I doing here?*

She glanced up into the rearview mirror to reassure herself about her appearance, then got out of the car and left the garage. She walked down a narrow passage and reached the side door, which she unlocked without incident. Taking a deep breath, she entered.

A narrow hall led into the interior of the house and Alexa hurried past closed doors on both sides, half expecting someone to jerk one open at any moment and challenge her presence.

A waiting silence greeted her as she reached an atrium more spacious than her whole apartment. Dark

Mediterranean-style furniture and marble floors harmonized with white walls. Alabaster sculptures and beautifully framed artwork were displayed in artistic arrangements like a formal gallery.

This was Mia's home.

Alexa was stunned by the opulence and grandeur of the rooms she glimpsed through arched doorways. Beautiful and sterile. No signs of carelessly flung books or belongings. Everything precisely in its place. Not a home, Alexa realized, just a place for show. Nothing to indicate that a loving family lived there.

Poor Mia, thought Alexa. They had been born of the same mother, shared the genetic pool of their ancestors, but by some quirk of choice, Mia had been adopted by affluent parents and Alexa by middle-class people. *I was the lucky one,* Alexa mused, understanding for the first time that Mia needed her as much as she needed her sister. Life had cheated them in different ways.

A wide, curving staircase rose majestically to a wide landing, turned and disappeared. Faint sounds floated from somewhere deep in the house. The kitchen, probably, Alexa decided as she quickly mounted the stairs. The only other sounds were her whispered footsteps on the deep wine carpet. She kept looking over the banister, searching for any sign that someone was watching her from below. She reached the upstairs hall with her chest rising and falling with quickened breath.

"The nursery is on your left at the far end of the house." The echo of Mia's voice was like an encouraging hand gently urging her forward. She walked down the hall and stopped in front of a closed door.

A thousand doubts assaulted her. What if the baby wasn't in the nursery? Maybe Dorrie had already awakened from her nap. The nanny could be tending to her. Alexa took a shaky breath and mentally upbraided herself. There wasn't time for any delay. She had to get the baby out of the house quickly. Leo could decide to come home and confront Mia at any moment.

I'm Mia. She straightened her back, turned the doorknob and pushed the door open. Her eyes traveled around the pretty pink nursery with its coordinating white furniture. The baby's crib was on the far wall, and with relief Alexa saw a rounded mound in the middle of it.

Thank God for soap-opera addiction, thought Alexa as melodramatic dialogue from a television set floated in from the other room. Mia's reassurances had been true. Everything was just as she had said.

Alexa hurried to the crib. The baby lay asleep on her tummy with her little arms in a relaxed position above her fair head. A fringe of delicate eyelashes rested on her smooth cheeks. A rosebud mouth and tiny pink fingernails matched the rose color of a soft baby blanket. Dorrie was more precious than her pictures—and Alexa was scared to death of her. She'd never had anything to do with babies, let alone one that looked so helpless and fragile. What if Dorrie started screaming when she picked her up? The baby's cries would bring the nanny running.

Hurry. Hurry. The command came from some sharp and loud inner voice. Alexa bent over, slipped her hands under the sleeping infant and lifted her up. The baby gave a warning whimper, but didn't open her eyes. Alexa clumsily adjusted her grip, trying to keep the blanket from slipping to the floor as she tightened her hold on the baby.

She started across the room, intending to call out to the nanny when she was closer to the door. Before she reached it, she heard the television go off. The next minute, a woman's voice sounded behind her.

"Oh, Mrs. Santini. I didn't know you'd come back. I guess it's time to leave, all right. The cars should be here any minute. Don't you want me to take the baby while you—"

Alexa shook her head and without turning around said over her shoulder, "No, thank you, Clara."

"I'll get my things and be right down," the woman called after her.

With the baby clutched to her breast, Alexa hurried down the hall to the main staircase. She quickly descended the steps, but before she reached the bottom one, her heart plummeted to her feet.

The double front door stood open. A butler and a young maid were carrying suitcases outside to a parked limousine. A burly square-faced chauffeur began loading them in the trunk of the long white car.

"I'm supposed to leave for a private resort upstate." Mia's words came back to Alexa with the warning clang of a fire bell. That's what the nanny was talking about. In a minute Clara would be downstairs, ready to leave.

Alexa took the remaining steps at a reckless speed and spun around the bottom newel post on her heels. She fled with the baby down the side hall. Thank heavens all the activity was at the front of the house. There was a good chance she could slip into the garage and drive away in Mia's car. She'd leave everyone puzzled, but she was positive no would be alerted to the impersonation as she sped by in the BMW.

She opened the door and cautiously stepped outside. The passageway to the garage was empty. She could hear voices coming from the front of the house. The baby was still asleep in her arms, thank heavens.

Alexa had almost reached the garage, when footsteps sounded behind her. She kept moving. Her heart lodged in her throat. Should she try to run for it? The instinct to bolt was almost overpowering.

"There you are, Mrs. Santini. I was looking for you," a man's voice said from behind her.

What should she do?

The footsteps quickened. "Mrs. Santini..."

What should she do? She couldn't pretend she hadn't heard. *You're Mia. Don't panic. Act natural.* With a force of will, she stopped. She took a deep breath and turned around. Then her knees buckled as if someone had landed a fist in the pit of her stomach.

The man coming toward her was in a tweed jacket and his bold face was framed by black hair. She stared at him in utter disbelief. It couldn't be—but it was! *He was the same man who had been in Guy's apartment.*

Chapter Three

Alexa took a step backward. She had the distinct impression that he'd been waiting for her in the garage. Brazen brown eyes under jet black eyelashes stared directly into her face. The force of his scrutiny was like a devil's wind whipping around her. All warmth drained from her face and instinctively her arms tightened on the baby.

"I'm sorry...did I startle you?" he asked.

But nothing in his tone was apologetic and arctic-cold eyes stabbed her with an intensity that sent weakness flooding into her legs. The steellike hardness of his muscular body suggested a boxing ring and one glance at his broad hands warned her that they could fasten on her like iron manacles. Did he recognize her for the fraud that she was? Her lips were dry and it was all she could do not to duck her head and run. To hide her fear, she kept her expression as haughty as possible as she glared at him.

"What do you want?" she demanded in as strong a voice as her terror-filled chest would allow.

The stony lines of his mouth and chin softened slightly, as if he were amused by her autocratic behavior.

"Let me introduce myself, Mrs. Santini. I'm Damas Silva, your new bodyguard. I'll be accompanying you on your vacation."

New bodyguard. Guy's replacement? Vacation?

His stabbing scrutiny never left her face. What should she do? Stand her ground? Confess that she wasn't Mia? Try to explain why she was making off with the Santini baby? His enveloping nearness was like the charged air of lightning-filled thunderheads. The way he had introduced himself indicated he and Mia had never met. But he had been in Guy's apartment and he had found the earring. Was that why his expression bordered on cruel smugness? Damn him! A flush of anger brought warmth back into her cheeks. She had to bluff it out—she had no other choice.

"I don't understand, Mr. Silva," she said crisply. "What exactly is going on?"

Once again he seemed to find a sadistic humor in the arrogant lift of her chin.

"Your husband called me earlier . . . he wants me to see you safely to Foxfire Valley and watch over you till he arrives next Saturday. It's my pleasure, I assure you," he said, a mocking twist to those hard lips. "I've been working for your husband in a different capacity and this assignment will be an . . . interesting change."

"What happened to Guy?"

A flicker of a shadow crossed his eyes, but he said, "I really don't know, Mrs. Santini." His cold, measured tone denied the truth of his words.

During this exchange, Alexa had been nervously grasping the baby too tightly. Dorrie woke up with a lusty cry. She thrust her arms and legs out in every direction with a violent protest; suddenly a wild force, an exploding ball of energy. As the baby screamed at the top of her healthy lungs, Alexa clumsily shifted her about, completely at a loss how to quiet her. The squalling infant seemed to know better than anyone that she was not in her mother's arms.

"I think the cars are ready," said Damas above the infant's cries, and put a firm hand on Alexa's arm. He guided her around to the front of the house, where two cars stood waiting, the white limousine and a black Cadillac. The thickly built chauffeur who was standing by the limousine stiffened, shoved his cap on his bald head and quickly opened the car door.

At that moment, Clara came out of the house. Alexa saw that the nanny was a middle-aged overweight woman with an undefinable waistline. Her heavy features wore a scowl as she took the screaming baby from Alexa's arms.

"There, there, honey," she soothed. "It's time for your bottle." She gave Alexa a look of thinly veiled disgust before she turned around and disappeared quickly with the baby into the back seat of the second car.

Everything was happening too fast. Alexa couldn't stop the situation from reeling out of control.

"After you, Mrs. Santini," said Damas. He loomed over her and with a steel grip he put her into the back seat of the limousine, then shut the door on her be-wildered face. "Let's go, Malchek," he said to the driver, climbing into the front seat.

Frantic protests caught in Alexa's throat as they drove away from the house. What should she do? Scream and demand to be let out? What would happen then? Would they summon Leo Santini? Or would they just keep driving? Was the openly dangerous Damas secretly laughing at her? Did the ugly chauffeur know that the woman in the back seat wasn't his boss's wife? What was even more frightening was the possibility that her impersonation was so good that she was about to reap the consequences of her sister's infidelity.

A glass window separated Alexa from the men. The chauffeur's big head sat on his thick neck like that of a muscle-bound wrestler's, and the reflection of Malchek's ugly face as he glanced from time to time into the rearview mirror was enough to send cold chills washing over Alexa. Her fearful eyes fled to Damas Silva, sitting beside the driver. There was a cool arrogance about him that made him more frightening than the other man. Cold, hard and handsome, just the kind of man who cared little about anything but his own selfish agenda. He must be high in Leo Santini's favor, thought Alexa, someone the mob boss could trust to be impervious to Mia's feminine charms. From the moment the new bodyguard had met her at the side of the house, he had taken charge. He had successfully thrown her off her stride and put her in the car before she'd had time to think about the consequences.

One thing was certain, Alexa realized as she nervously clutched Mia's alligator bag. She couldn't go on pretending to be her sister. Even if by some miracle she had everyone fooled for the moment, the ruse couldn't possibly last. There was much more to impersonating someone than just looking like her. The brief glimpse into Mia's world had made Alexa painfully aware that her twin's values and hers were completely different.

The two might be mirror images of each other, but they would never react to people and situations in the same way. Alexa was glad that she had never met Leo Santini. Mia had said that her husband would never have allowed a friendship to develop between them. Alexa burned at the idea. No doubt, she would have let the mobster know what she thought of men who selfishly treated their women like possessions.

Somehow she had to get out of the dangerous charade without Santini finding out that Mia had a sister. If he didn't know about Alexa's existence, he wouldn't have a clue to his wife's whereabouts. Mia would be safe at Alexa's place until they decided what to do.

Alexa's thoughts raced. Their simple little plan had turned into a nightmare. Alexa eyed a cellular phone within easy reach of the back seat. No telling what her sister would do when she didn't return as planned. She might become hysterical when she learned that Alexa had failed to get the baby. *I did the best I could,* she thought defensively. Now she had to get herself out of the impersonation the quickest way she could. Mia had reassured Alexa that they had nothing to lose if the idea didn't work. They hadn't considered the possibility that it might work too well.

Would the men in the front seat be able to hear everything she said if she used the car phone? She didn't know if the intercom between the front and back was on or off. She decided to chance it.

She reached for the phone at the same instant that Damas Silva's dark head turned in her direction. His eyes stabbed her like a piercing stiletto. The challenging look made her feel utterly transparent, as if he'd read her intent.

She let her hand fall back in her lap. If he knew what kind of game she was playing, why didn't he come right out and confront her? Why was he going on with the charade if he realized she wasn't Mia? It didn't make sense, unless he had some sadistic plan to turn her over to Santini. Alexa suppressed a shiver. She'd never be able to protect Mia if that happened.

Before she could decide what to do, they had left the city and crossed the Hudson River via the George Washington Bridge, then turned onto the Palisades Parkway. Nervously she glanced out the back window. The black Cadillac followed a safe distance behind. She was trapped in a moving car speeding north on a divided highway. Somehow she'd have to get away before they reached the upstate resort. But how?

She glimpsed houses and towns through stands of trees on both sides of the road. Once before when she had traveled the Palisades Parkway, she had stopped at Patriot's Corner, a small shopping center just off the highway. As far as she could remember, this cluster of tourist shops, a gas station and large restaurant was about a forty-minute drive from where they were now.

Her mind raced. A desperate plan began to take shape. She'd order the driver to stop at Patriot's Corner. But would he? Of course he would—if he thought she was Mia. After all, both the men were employees. *And I'm Mrs. Santini.* Alexa swallowed hard. If they ignored her, she could feel certain that they knew she was an impersonator.

Her hands were clammy with cold sweat as the shopping center drew closer and closer. Patriot's Corner had been crowded the time that she had shopped there. Tourists pushing in and out of stores should make it easy for Mia Santini to disappear into the crowd. All she had to do, Alexa told herself, was pretend that she'd forgotten to bring something, go in one of the shops, buy a different set of clothes and slip out of the store with other shoppers. She'd have to figure out how to get back to the city. As soon as she could she'd phone Mia, explain what had happened. Her sister could call home, let them know she was all right, but not give away her whereabouts.

Alexa dreaded telling Mia that she had failed to get away with the baby. Everything had happened so fast. If only she had gotten out of the house five minutes earlier. If only— No use going over the whole fiasco. Anyway, she'd been close to pulling it off. There was some satisfaction in that. Now she'd have to get out of the masquerade as quickly as possible.

She opened Mia's purse to see how much money was in her sister's wallet. Only six dollars! She couldn't buy more than a pair of sunglasses with that. She dug out Mia's checkbook. It showed a generous bank balance and held a string of credit cards. The photo on Mia's driver's license was reassuring. No problem passing for her sister if she used it as identification. She had to have money to buy a change of clothes at the shopping center and to pay for some kind of transportation back to the city.

Alexa studied her sister's signature on the back of the credit cards. The handwriting was nothing like her own. She'd never be able to cash a check or use one of the credit cards unless she could forge Mia's name. She took out a small notebook and a gold pen and started practicing. Her sister would claim the signature as hers if anyone questioned it later, but a stern conscience reminded her that forgery was a felony and that every step in the impersonation brought her closer to the brink of possible arrest.

She clung to valid reasons why she shouldn't lean forward in the seat and admit the lie. She didn't know if such a confession would put Mia at risk. No telling what Leo would do if he found out that his wife had been trying to deceive him. No, she couldn't chance it. She'd play out the charade a little longer. Once she got away, no one would know where she'd gone and they'd all be safe.

She waited until the car was about a mile from Patriot's Corner and then she leaned forward in the seat. She didn't know whether she had to push a button on the intercom to talk to the driver or whether it was already on. She cleared her throat and coughed. Immediately Silva turned around with a raised, questioning eyebrow.

Thank heavens she hadn't given in to the impulse to call Mia. She knew then that the two men would have overheard every word she spoke into the car phone.

"I want to spend a few minutes at Patriot's Corner," she said as evenly as she could. "Pull into the restaurant parking lot." Her heart thumped loudly with every word.

The chauffeur shot Silva a disgusted look. In response, Damas just gave a slight shrug. *Did that mean they were going to do it?* She couldn't tell.

The next few minutes were an eternity. When they approached the shopping center, her heart almost stopped from rising apprehension. What would she do if they refused?

Malchek growled something and Silva turned around. "Do you want the Caddy to stop, too?"

For a moment Alexa didn't know what he was talking about and then she saw him glance out the back window. *Caddy! The black Cadillac.* She shook her head. "No."

He nodded, talked briefly into a cellular phone, and the Cadillac sped past them.

As Alexa watched the car disappear in the distance, she silently whispered *Goodbye, Dorrie.* A sense of utter loss brought a sickening twist to her stomach. Would she ever see her niece again? If what Mia said was true, Leo wouldn't hesitate to take the baby away from her mother—forever. A spurt of anger mingled with a wave of frustration. Damn it! She'd been so close to getting away with the baby. In a couple of minutes more she would have been in Mia's car and on the way back to her apartment. Now it was too late to do anything but get away as quickly as she could. The fact that Silva and the driver were obeying her order to stop at the shopping mall seemed to indicate that they had accepted her as Mrs. Santini—unless Mr.

Silva was just biding his time to expose her. What did he plan to do with the incriminating earring? He could be playing along with the impersonation for some nefarious reason of his own. His hard, mocking smile hinted that he enjoyed seeing her squirm.

The limousine slowed, exited the parkway and turned into a shopping complex built in a half circle, with a restaurant located at one end and a gas station at the other. The chauffeur drove into a parking space at the side of the restaurant as Alexa had instructed.

So far, so good, she thought as both men got out. Silva stood by the car, his dark eyes played over the restaurant and parking lot. Malchek went around and opened the back door of the limousine. The chauffeur's cold gray eyes raked Alexa as she got out and she could feel animosity as thick as mist coming from him. Was it for her—or Mia?

She avoided looking directly at him or Silva. "I want to do a little shopping. I need to pick up a few things I forgot." And then in a tone she often used to instruct her students, she added, "Please wait for me in the restaurant." She walked away without looking back.

Damas leaned up against the car and watched her cross the parking lot. He'd trained himself to recognize trouble and this was one gal who fitted the word in every sense. Somebody ought to knock some sense into her. She was the kind who could tie a man up in knots and enjoy witnessing his contortions as he tried to get free. She had a natural graceful swing to her hips that was enough to trigger lustful thoughts in any man and the damnedest blue eyes he'd ever seen. He gave a short laugh. They had hardly left the city and she was up to something. *All right, sweetheart, let the games begin.*

Alexa fought the urge to turn around to check if either one of the men was following her. The sidewalk was as crowded with shoppers as she had remembered, and she tried to keep her stride casual until she reached the door of a ladies' boutique. She stopped, looked back. No sign of either men in the throng coming toward her.

She ducked inside the shop. For several moments, she stood half-hidden behind a rack of sundresses, watching the door.

"May I help you?"

A buxom saleswoman with dyed red hair came up behind Alexa. Her suspicious expression clearly indicated that she viewed Alexa as a possible shoplifter.

"Are you interested in our sundresses?"

"No. A pair of cords...blue...size nine." Alexa turned to a rack of wildly colored T-shirts. "And one of these in a large." She pointed to a red one with a pair of tropical birds painted in bold colors on the front. The gaudy top would cover her figure nicely.

"Large?" questioned the woman.

"It's not for me," Alexa lied. The saleslady followed her around with a perplexed frown on her face as Alexa picked out a cheap pair of plastic sandals, a straw sun hat, and a pair of dark glasses. The woman eyed Mia's pure silk blouse, designer skirt and expensive shoes. Alexa could see her mentally shaking her head.

"Will that be all?" the saleswoman asked with a mechanical smile.

"Yes."

"Charge or cash?"

"Charge." Alexa drew out one of Mia's credit cards.

"Do you have a second piece of identification? Driver's license?"

"Yes." Alexa handed it to her.

"Everything correct?" Her eyes skimmed the personal data.

"Yes." *Except for one detail—it's not mine.*

The woman studied her as she handed back the license and then gave her the charge slip to sign. Had the saleslady's sixth sense told her something was wrong? Alexa knew that her behavior had been suspicious from the beginning, and her purchases were incongruous with the tasteful and expensive clothes she was wearing. Who could blame the woman for her doubts.

The pen felt alien in Alexa's hand. Her own handwriting was a full, easy-flowing script, but Mia's was tight, with a marked back slant. She tried to picture the signature in her mind's eye as she forged her sister's name. Had she been too deliberate as she'd signed the slip? Had her intense concentration given her away?

Her mouth was dry as she handed the slip back to the clerk. At that moment, the telephone rang. Alexa couldn't control a rise of panic as the woman stood there with the charge slip in her hand and answered a dozen questions about a special sale on panty hose.

Hurry. Hurry. Alexa shifted from one nervous foot to the other. Other customers were lining up behind her and still the saleswoman kept talking on the phone.

Alexa looked around for the fitting room while she waited for the clerk to get off the phone. *Blast it all!* Several customers were queuing for their turn to try on clothes. She couldn't lose that much time waiting. Every minute counted. The gas station! She'd change in the rest room. With her hair tucked up under the hat, her face clean of makeup, and wearing sloppy tourist clothes, she could mingle unnoticed in the crowd. She'd find a telephone and call Mia. After that, she'd decide the best way to get back home.

The redheaded saleslady finally hung up. She stared for a moment at the charge slip, as if trying to remember where she was. Then she tore the slip apart and gave Alexa her copy. She carefully put all the purchases in a plastic bag and was about to hand it across the counter to Alexa, when a man's hand reached out for the sack.

"Let me carry that for you, Mrs. Santini."

Chapter Four

For a shocked moment, Alexa didn't know what to do. Her first impulse was to grab the bag from Damas Silva's hand and run. *Steady. Don't panic.* She heard a voice that must have been her own say "Thank you." Without looking at him, she turned and headed out the store.

His long stride matched her hurried steps with ease. Several women shoppers passing by gave him a lingering smile and a buxom gal in tight stretch pants brazenly bumped into him. He responded with an amused chuckle and brushed past her.

Conceited, thought Alexa as she glimpsed his six-foot reflection in the store windows. He probably had all kinds of women drooling over his handsome dark profile and muscular physique. She had to admit he exuded a male magnetism that might have caught her attention under different circumstances, but as they walked side by side, he cast a shadow over her like a bird of prey. If she ran, he would be on her heels. If she tried to hide, he would find her. She was caught in a treacherous net of impersonation and the more she struggled the tighter the tangled cords holding her became. She'd never known raw fear before, but at that moment she felt the ruthless and vicious power of Leo Santini and the kind of men he hired. There was little doubt in Alexa's mind that Damas Silva had already proven his loyalty to the Santini interest.

He casually glanced at his watch. "Almost noon. Time for lunch."

She didn't answer. Mentally floundering about what to do next, she decided lunch was a good idea, not because her stomach was receptive to food, but because she needed time to think. Somehow she had to get away while they were stopped there at the shopping center. Once in the car again, she might have lost the only opportunity to slip away before her true identity was detected. She couldn't go on pretending to be Mia for very long. She was amazed she hadn't made some horrendous faux pas already.

As they walked, Damas was aware of the myriad expressions that flickered across her face like wild birds in flight. He had thwarted whatever plans she had made to ditch him and he could tell she was not about to admit defeat. Her breasts rose and fell in tantalizing rhythm with her quick steps. Her head high, her shoulders back and her arms swinging lightly at her sides made him aware once more of the natural feminine grace of her body. He wouldn't be surprised if she tried to use her seductive charms, looking at him with those mesmerizing blue eyes while her kissable lips pleaded for him to understand why she didn't want to go to Foxfire. He understood, all right. She had other plans, and they didn't include a husband.

When they reached the restaurant there was a line of people waiting for a table. "I wonder how long we'll be here," Alexa said, instantly calculating if she could use the delay to her advantage.

"No problem," he assured her. "I reserved a table while you were shopping."

He doesn't miss a beat, she thought angrily. His blasted efficiency was like a tight leash around her neck, controlling her every minute, pulling her back if she ventured too far away from his side.

"How thoughtful," she said, unable to keep the edge of sarcasm from her tone.

"I thought you'd be ready for lunch. After your shopping and all." He gave her one of his sardonic half smiles.

She longed to smack his supercilious face, but she held her temper. She was in a situation where she had to go against her own nature in order to protect her sister. And what did she know about the world Mia lived in? Almost nothing. She'd had only glimpses into her sister's closely guarded life. A single word or action and she could blow the impersonation. One thing was certain—Damas Silva was shrewd and calculating. Alexa knew she wouldn't be able to fool him for long. She was like someone skating on the edge of cracking ice, knowing that at any moment it was going to give way.

The hostess quickly led them to a small table at the far side of the restaurant. Damas held out a chair for her, his bold eyes offering an unspoken challenge.

"Thank you," she said coolly as she sat down. As he slipped the chair forward, his fingers accidentally or deliberately brushed against her shoulders and the back of her neck began to tingle. For an absurd moment she fantasized that he was going to press his lips against her nape. She felt herself go hot, and when he moved around the table and took a chair opposite her, she couldn't look at him.

"Is something the matter?" he asked.

"Not at all." She wasn't about to admit that she was even aware of his subtle sexual maneuvers. She was still fuming that he had scuttled her plans to change clothes and disappear in the crowd. Defeat didn't sit well with her. He thought he was dealing with a submissive wife, but he was going to discover how wrong he was when he suddenly found himself with no one to guard.

She glanced out a window that overlooked the parking lot and saw Malchek standing by the limousine, smoking. He looked up and met her eyes with an expression so malevolent that it chilled her to the bone.

A waitress handed them menus. Alexa stared at hers for a moment and then shot Damas a quick glance as she stood up. "Order me a Caesar salad and iced tea. I'll be back in a minute."

She walked away from the table and headed toward the ladies' room. Her hopes of an exit along the way rapidly faded. The rest rooms were in a dead-end hall. No way out of the building in that direction. She stopped in front of the door marked Ladies, glanced back down the hall, expecting to see Damas sauntering after her, but there was no sign that he had followed her.

A couple of pay phones were mounted on the wall just beyond the rest-room doors. She fished in Mia's purse for a quarter and quickly dialed her apartment.

Mia answered on the first ring. "Alexa. Thank heavens it's you. I've been so worried. What happened? Did you get the baby? Where are you? Why didn't—"

"Mia! Listen. Things didn't go the way we planned." She heard her sister's quick intake of breath. "I'm at Patriot's Corner Shopping Center, off the Palisades Parkway."

"What on earth? Oh, my God," she wailed. "What are you doing there? Where's my baby? Didn't you get her?"

"I made it inside the house and up to the nursery. The baby was asleep and the nanny was watching TV, just as you said. I took Dorrie and Clara didn't object."

"Then what happened? Why didn't you bring her to me as we discussed? Did somebody recognize you?"

"No... at least, I don't think so. And that may be the problem. Your husband sent a new bodyguard to the house to replace Guy. He stopped me just as I was leaving with the baby. I didn't know what to do. Dorrie started screaming her head off. Before I knew it, the new bodyguard ushered me into the limo waiting to take you to the resort."

"Dorrie! What about Dorrie?"

"She's with her nanny... in the other car. The Caddy went on, but I made the chauffeur of the limo stop here." There wasn't time to go into the forged credit slip and her aborted plan to change clothes. Silva could come down the hall any minute. "Mia, I've got to get out of this impersonation—"

"No, you can't. You have to go get Dorrie."

"I told you. The baby and Clara have already gone ahead. I'm sorry, Mia, really I am. I did my best."

There was a heavy silence on the line and then Mia said, "No one at the resort knows me. We've never been there before. Alexa, once you get there, you can easily slip away with the baby just as we planned."

"Mia, listen to me. I have to get away before anyone knows who I really am. Once your husband finds out you have a sister, he'll know where you are—"

"I don't care," she cried. "If I can't have my baby, I don't care what happens to me."

"Mia, don't talk nonsense."

"I mean it, Alexa. I can't live without Dorrie. I'll kill myself—"

"Stop it, Mia."

"If Leo takes Dorrie away from me, my life will be over."

Her voice was suddenly calm enough to make Alexa's skin prickle.

"I'd rather be dead."

"You don't mean that," Alexa countered, but Mia's threat of suicide rang true. She was an abused wife, emotionally if not physically, and the loss of her baby could send her over the edge.

"You don't know what my life is like. Without Dorrie, there's nothing...nothing."

Alexa heard the desperation in her voice. "You have to believe me. I'll kill myself."

"I can't go on being you, Mia."

"Please try. Oh, please, Alexa, don't give up." She wailed hysterically.

Her sister's volatile emotions frightened her. What if she carried out her threat? The image of Mia lying dead in her apartment was all too real. *How could I live with myself if that happened?* Alexa knew she couldn't. She had always prided herself on being able to do what was needed, despite any unpleasantness. Her cowardice would taunt her forever. Continuing the impersonation was madness but she had to try. "All right, Mia I'll see what I can do."

"I'll never forget what you're doing for me," Mia sobbed. "You're wonderful. No one has ever cared before."

"I can't promise anything, Mia, but I'll do my best. I have no idea what will happen when we get to the resort." Her mouth was suddenly dry. She wanted to tell Mia about Damas Silva and the way he was guarding her like a bulldog. She was afraid he would hand over the damning earring first thing when Leo arrived at the resort. What if she couldn't get away before that? What would the mobster do if she was caught impersonating his wife? She wanted to ask about Malchek's open animosity. But she didn't. "I can't talk anymore, Mia. Call Mrs. Trimble in the apartment downstairs." Alexa gave her the number of a retired lady who loved to mother people. "She'll take care of you. I'll telephone you again when I get to the resort. Don't worry."

"I love you, Alexa."

"I love you, too." Her eyes were moist as she hung up and hurried into the ladies' room.

She stood in front of the sink and stared at her unfamiliar reflection in the mirror. She longed to wash the heavy makeup from her eyes, brush her fair hair back into a casual ponytail and wipe the deep red lipstick from her mouth. She wanted to be herself again.

Every core of her being rebeled at the part she had to play. She never allowed herself to be pushed around by anyone, especially arrogant, conceited males who expected every female to fall at their feet.

She thought about the way Damas Silva birddogged her every step and at the back of her mind was an insane desire to outwit him at every turn. He'd be in big trouble with Santini if he suddenly found himself with no one to guard. He could show Leo the earring for all she cared, once she and the baby were safely out of his reach.

She took a small cosmetic bag out of Mia's purse. She was surprised to find her hands quite steady. Now that the decision had been made, she geared herself for the challenges ahead. She freshened her lipstick, brushed the soft ringlets around her face, touched a powder puff to her nose. Satisfied with the result, she straightened her slim shoulders, and with her chin jutted at a confident angle she walked to the rest-room door and opened it. For some reason she wasn't surprised to see Silva waiting for her.

"There you are. I was beginning to wonder," he said.

If he was worried she might have given him the slip, he could relax—for the moment. She brushed by him without answering and headed back to their table.

DAMAS WATCHED her peck at her salad. Her thoughts were miles away—he could tell that. She wanted to skip out on him—he knew that. Hell, she was as tense as someone holding a hot wire. Worried about her lover, no doubt. He'd peeked at the stuff she'd bought in the store. No question about it. She intended some kind of a disappearing act. He'd known from the beginning that she wanted to get away from the house with the baby. Waiting around for her husband at some resort wasn't in her plans.

He leaned back in his chair and sipped his coffee. Her little ploy to stop at the shopping center had been painfully clear. Had she really believed he'd let her waltz off like that? He'd made sure that he kept her in view through the windows of the store. He'd almost felt sorry for her when he appeared at her side and took the package.

When she'd abruptly left the table, he let her go. He'd already made certain there was no exit down that hall. When she was slow coming back to the table, he'd asked the waitress to check on her, and was told she was on the phone.

It figured. Trying to find out what happened to Guy Lentz, no doubt. She was something else, this gal. Having fun and games right under her husband's nose. Not that Santini rated very high as a husband. Everyone knew that he treated his wife like a paid employee. But Guy had been stupid to get involved. Fooling around with the boss's wife was an expressway to a short life. The poor jerk was probably on his way to an arranged fatal accident.

When Damas had been summoned to Leo's office that morning, he wasn't told anything except that he was being assigned as Mia Santini's bodyguard. His instructions were to go to the house and accompany her to the Foxfire Resort in upstate New York. That was all. Everyone knew that Guy Lentz was deeply in debt to the bookies. Was that what this was all about? Or had Santini found out about his wife's little affair? Damas never liked to go into a job without knowing all the facts, so on his own, he'd gone to Guy's apartment, and when he'd found the rumpled bed and diamond earring, he'd known why the bodyguard was being replaced.

When he got to the house, he'd found Mrs. Santini trying to slip out the side door with the baby. It was plain that she was taking a powder now that her little affair had blown up in her face. He'd gotten there just in time to stop her, but he knew that she hadn't given up. She was determined to get away from him—that was clear.

He watched her across the table. She kept her eyes lowered and her hand trembled slightly as she lifted her coffee cup. The little lady was scared. And she had every right to be. He felt bad for her, but his boss wanted her at the resort and that's where she was going. Women like Mia Santini deserved what they got. An imbedded anger surfaced. He had been only eight years old when his mother had run off with a fellow who operated a trucking business. His father had tried to excuse her, telling Damas that things weren't always as they seemed, but he'd known even then that some women sacrificed everything for their own pleasure. The gal sitting across the table from him was one of them.

"Not hungry?" he asked.

She started at the sound of his voice. "No, I...I never eat much when I'm traveling."

"You and Mr. Santini travel quite a bit?"

She nodded and abruptly set down her cup, spilling coffee into the saucer.

"Weren't you in Spain last year? Your second wedding anniversary, wasn't it?" She visibly tensed. Not a good subject. He didn't know why he brought it up. Something about her riled him. An unspoken challenge of some kind. He'd be damned if this gal was going to pull him around like some lackey.

She gave him a look as stony as his. "Have you worked for... for my husband very long?"

"Eight or nine months," he said.

"Doing what?"

"Various things. Your husband is a man of many interests, Mrs. Santini. Nothing is routine. I've never been bored with any assignment."

"Until now, perhaps?"

He smiled at her directness. "Frankly, I'm finding it more interesting than I expected."

"In what way?"

She was digging beneath his words. Maybe she was sharper than what showed on the surface.

"A change of scenery and all that." *Aren't you looking forward to your vacation, now that your lover won't be around to share it?* Those smoky blue eyes of hers were wide and beautiful—and as dangerous as quicksand. He could see how she could get to a man, all right. "Are you ready to go?"

A muscle flickered in her cheek. Fear? Anger? He found himself intrigued. What was going on behind those depthless blue eyes? She was trying to run out on her husband, the little fool. And that wasn't going to happen. He sure as hell wasn't going to jeopardize his standing with Santini by bumbling this bodyguard job. He'd worked too hard to impress the boss. It had taken the shooting of a federal agent to get his attention, and now that he had it, no two-timing wife was going to ruin his chances to move up in the organization. He'd stay as close to her as a Siamese twin if he had to.

They walked back to the limousine without talking. Malchek dutifully opened the back door, but it was obvious he didn't have any use for his boss's wife, thought Damas. The ugly man didn't like her and he didn't bother to hide it.

"I'll sit in back with Mrs. Santini for the rest of the trip," Damas told him.

The chauffeur's woolly eyebrows matted over his thick nose and his tone was almost a sneer. "Yes, sir."

The lady wasn't pleased about the arrangement, either, but she seemed unsure about ordering him to ride in the front, as he had before. She sat as close to the far side of the seat as she could, refusing to look at him as the car sped northward. His nearness clearly annoyed her. He smiled to himself. *Get used to it, little lady.*

"The Hudson Valley is pretty this time of year, isn't it?" He found a malicious pleasure in bringing up a mundane subject. "The city's hot even in June."

She turned and gave him a pointed glare that should have withered any further attempts at social conversation, but Damas only silently chuckled. "I bet you're really going to enjoy yourself, Mrs. Santini. Your husband knows how to go first class. This Foxfire place must really be something. Have you been there before?"

He watched her chest rise and fall in a deep breath. Her voice was a little unsteady when she responded.

"Do you mind? I have a headache."

"Oh, sorry."

She leaned back and closed her eyes. Her expression remained tense. Damas watched her. He'd bet anything that her mind was working at full speed. He fingered the earring in his pocket. Maybe that's what she'd been on the phone about. She must be panicked about losing it. No wonder she had a headache. Her lover was in Santini's hands and her husband wanted her kept under guard until he joined her. Not a pretty picture.

Damas would have preferred to be doing anything but riding herd on some guy's wayward wife. Why had Santini picked him for the job? Why not someone older who had been in the organization longer? Something didn't feel right. His sixth sense was vibrating like a lightning rod. And he'd kept alive trusting his instincts. He was going to—

Without warning a rear tire on the limo blew. Alexa cried out as the car careened dangerously. She was thrown forward, off balance, and Damas grabbed her to keep her in the seat. For a brief second his hands closed on the softness of her waist and brushed against the swelling softness of her breasts. As he pulled her back into the seat, her hair grazed his cheek, and its perfume triggered his desire like a gentle caress. He could feel the sweet length of her body pressed back against his and a warning went off in his head. He abruptly set her on her side of the seat.

"It's all right. Just a flat," he said gruffly. "Malchek will change the tire and we'll be on our way again."

The chauffeur swore as he climbed out of the car and slammed his door in disgust.

"I thought...I thought someone was shooting at us."

He smiled at her naïveté. Bullets spraying a car sounded a lot different from a blowout. If it had been a gunshot, he would have had her on the floor and his .38 out before the limo had stopped. Splintered glass, twisted metal and groans of pain were fresh memories. His reflexes were finely honed.

They sat in silence for several minutes. She sat rigidly on her side of the seat and he stretched his long legs out in front in a relaxed position. He wasn't about to let her see how aware he was of her seductive nearness. He put his head back on the cushion and closed his eyes.

Suddenly she announced, "I want to get out."

He straightened up and quickly looked around. They had just turned onto Route 6, and were crossing Bear Mountain State Park. Pine trees covered rolling hills and thick groves of birch trees, maples, oaks and dogwoods hugged both sides of the road. A small stream ran through dark gray rocky outcrops. He'd have a hard time keeping her in sight if she decided to run for it. But where would she go? Was she stupid enough to think some taxi would be coming along later to pick her up? He doubted if she'd ever had on a pair of hiking boots in her life and those spindly high heels wouldn't last a hundred yards. In some way he wished she'd spring for it. Serve her right.

He held the door open for her. A brisk wind caught her hair and trailed soft strands across her face. She raised a hand to push them back from her forehead and then gave up. She took a few steps away from the car and then stood motionless on a grassy strip at the edge of the road. A blue jay rose from the bushes, dipped and soared, filling the air with its squawking cry. She followed it with her eyes until it disappeared and then stood with her arms folded over her chest, staring at some undetermined point on a nearby hill.

Damas leaned up against the car and watched her. As the wind whipped against her soft blouse, molding her feminine curves, a pained expression deepened lines around her sensuous mouth. Worrying about Guy, no doubt. Their affair must have been hot and heavy. Stupid. Never let a gal get under your skin like that. He'd had plenty of chances, but women were dangerous in this business. Even a gal like Mia Santini wasn't worth the gamble. Guy should have been smarter. Tumbling the boss's wife amounted to a death wish.

Mia walked a little way toward the small stream. Damas followed. What was going on in that pretty head of hers? Did she think she could jump that stream and get away? She'd never make it across. She'd land in the middle of it for sure. That would be a sight to see...her shiny hair dripping with water, her blouse clinging to her like wet paper and—

She turned around. "Why are you looking at me like that?"

"Like what?" he parried, angry with himself and with her. What could she expect a man to think, when that blasted tight skirt showed off long, supple legs and a rounded behind that begged for a man's touch?

He deliberately let his eyes travel down to the short hem of her skirt and back again.

He could see the heat rising in her face. She clenched her fists at her side as if resisting the urge to slap his face.

"I'm going for a walk."

He grabbed her arm. "No, I think Malchek is about finished with the tire. We don't want to be too late getting to the resort, do we?"

She pulled her arm away. Her eyes blazed like blue hot coals for a minute and then the fire went out and a dark shadow was present. She nodded. "No, we don't. The sooner the better."

Chapter Five

When the limousine passed through a security gate at the Foxfire Resort, Alexa glimpsed the kind of luxurious complex she had only seen in magazines. Nestled in a mountain glen beside a small lake, an elegant hotel rose eight stories to a jagged roofline of cupolas and towers. Formal gardens laced with brick paths and numerous stone terraces overlooked a lush green golf course and sapphire swimming pool. Masses of shrubs and flowers blended with drifts of evergreens and low shrubs mounting upward on the nearby hillsides.

The natural beauty and elegant accommodations were lost on Alexa. Something like hysterical laughter caught in her throat as she viewed the secluded resort. Her plan to snatch Dorrie from this place struck Alexa as idiotic enough to be almost funny. What on earth had she been thinking of to agree to such a wildly impossible scheme? Mia hadn't been to the resort, so she didn't know how isolated the place was. Her sister had made it sound like a simple thing to keep the impersonation going a little longer. Now what was Alexa going to do? Trying to continue to be Mia Santini once they entered the hotel was utter insanity. Why on earth had she ever agreed?

"I'll kill myself." A taunting inner voice reminded Alexa that nothing had changed. Mia teetered on the edge of emotional collapse. And even if Alexa decided not to go on with the impersonation, confessing to the deception was a two-edged sword. At the moment, no one knew where Mia was. Once it became known that she had a twin sister, Alexa's apartment would no longer be a safe hiding place. Leo could drag Mia away in the same forceful way his men had taken Guy. And in the second place, Alexa didn't want to think about what Santini would do to her for having tried to dupe him.

As the car circled a drive to the front of the hotel, Alexa realized with sickening certainty that she had gone beyond the point of no return in her impersonation.

"What's the matter? Don't you like what you see?" Damas asked, his dark eyes watching her face.

What if she said, *I don't want to stay here. I want to go back to the city.* What if she demanded that Malchek turn the car around and head back to New York? The flickering smile on Damas's face would undoubtedly break into a broad grin. He had his orders. Leo Santini wanted his wife at Foxfire and the two men in his employment would see to it that she was there when he joined her in a few days. *I'll have to get away before then.*

"Is this your first stay at Foxfire?" Damas asked.

"Yes." That was certainly true. She'd never come close to staying at such an exclusive resort.

"It's not grand enough for your liking?" he prodded with a mocking edge to the words.

He must have picked up on her inner recoil as she'd reacted to the extreme privacy of the place.

"I'm sure you'll find it bearable," he added.

It was obvious that he thought she was displeased with the looks of the resort. She wanted to cram his sarcastic retort down his throat, but she held her fury. She had nothing to gain by challenging his attitude. He had made it clear that he was doing a job that didn't please him much. All indications were that he accepted her as Santini's unfaithful wife. He thought he was guarding Mia, she mused with satisfaction, and that made him the dope.

She wondered if she should try to get the earring from him. One look at his set jaw and hard cheekbones checked that idea. She didn't want any confrontations with him, but she didn't know how she could endure his presence for even one more minute. He disturbed her in more ways than she wanted to admit. The brief physical contact they'd had when the tire had blown was unlike anything she'd experienced before. His fleeting touch upon her breasts and waist had kindled an instant infusion of heat. When he had pulled her back against him, she had felt safe. Protected, not frightened. As absurd as it was, she wanted his arms to enfold her and hold her tight. Luckily, he'd abruptly set her away before she lost her mind completely.

The big car rolled to a stop under the front awning, and immediately two young men in blue-and-gold uniforms appeared and stood waiting for instructions. Damas helped Alexa out of the car. She looked past the doorman and into the beckoning lobby. A wave of fright sent an icy weakness surging through her. *I can't go on with this. I can't!*

She must have wavered, because Damas tightened his grip on her arm. His eyes narrowed, and from his stony gaze, she knew it was futile to do anything but try to cope with the situation as best she could. She'd have to carry on the impersonation for a little longer. Once she was in the privacy of her room, she would be able to think more clearly. The thought strengthened her. In a few minutes she'd be alone, away from him, from his measuring eyes and that sardonic curve of his mouth, which both infuriated and frightened her.

As they crossed the lobby and approached the registration desk, Alexa waited for someone to point an accusing finger at her. Several fashionably dressed women gave her the once-over as they sauntered past her. A couple of men offered a welcoming smile. Her heartbeat quickened. *Maybe some of the guests knew Mia.* What would she do if an acquaintance of the Santinis tried to engage her in conversation? She had no clue what kind of chitchat was appropriate. How could she fake talking about places and people that were completely beyond her experience?

Alexa's breath was tight in her chest as they approached the registration desk. She was relieved when Damas took charge. He gave her name to the desk clerk. A small man with a toothbrush mustache and thinning gray hair nodded officiously and gave Alexa a plastic smile.

"Welcome to Foxfire, Mrs. Santini. We hope that you and your husband will enjoy your stay with us."

He handed an electronic key to an aging bellman. "Take Mrs. Santini to the Alpine Suite."

Damas lingered a moment at the desk, while Alexa followed the man across the spacious lobby. They passed huge bouquets of fresh flowers that perfumed the air with a delicate sweetness. A ribbed ceiling rose high above a mezzanine that overlooked the lobby. Several people stood at the railing, looking down, and Alexa felt horribly on display. She kept her eyes straight ahead as she passed conversational groupings of chairs, sofas and tables that dotted the marble floor. She was afraid to meet anyone's eyes, fearing to see that start of recognition that would plunge her further into the nightmare.

The bellman led her past the main elevators to one discreetly placed in a small hall. Just before the elevator doors closed, Damas stepped in beside her. Her heart plummeted. How could she possibly get away if he continued to be her constant shadow?

IN A CORNER of the lobby, Malchek watched as the elevator doors closed. Then he turned and walked to an alcove of telephones. His thick fingers quickly punched the numbers for a collect call.

"Yeah, boss. It's me. The new guy's on the job... yeah, I got my eyes open. Don't worry. If she takes to him, I'll know it. Sure, gotcha. How soon you coming? Right. She's acting funny, all right. Like she'll take a powder the first chance she gets. Don't worry, she'll be here. She ain't getting away with nothin'." He hung up the receiver and grunted, "Not a damn thing."

As the elevator sped upward, Alexa stood stiffly beside Damas. Every time she was close to him the air was charged like the sky before a summer storm. Her eyes flickered to the wave of raven hair hanging over his brow and the molded strength of his cheeks and chin. All right, he was good-looking and he intrigued her, she admitted defensively, but blast it all, she didn't need the aggravation of a sexually attractive strong-armed bodyguard. "Where's your room?"

"On the same floor as your suite...next door, in fact. So I'll be close by if you need me," he said solemnly.

Next door. How would she ever manage to get by him? He was like a cobra, curled ready to spring if she made a wrong move. Her mind raced. Nighttime. That was her only hope. She couldn't make any kind of a move until she was sure he was asleep. And Dorrie. Somehow she'd have to snatch the baby out from under the nanny's nose. There had been a couple of taxis and an airport shuttle at the entrance when they had arrived. Once she had the baby she'd have to find transportation or hike out of the place to the highway and try to catch a ride into Grandview, the nearest town. Getting away from Damas was the first challenge. He was the razor edge between success and failure.

She kept her eyes away from his cool, scrutinizing face. He seemed to have an uncanny ability to read her thoughts, and his nearness was like sandpaper on her raw nerves.

When the elevator doors swung open, they stepped out into a spacious sitting-room area with thick carpets and comfortable furniture for lounging. Straight ahead in the middle of a long wall, a pair of carved double ivory doors faced the elevator—obviously the entrance to the suite. As Alexa stepped farther out into the sitting room, she saw tall windows overlooking the grounds and lake on her left, and opposite them, in the middle of the wall to the right of the elevator, there were two doors to other rooms.

Her stomach took a sickening plunge. *Both those rooms would have a clear view of the sitting area and the elevator if the doors were left opened.*

The sound of a baby crying mingled with the blare of a television coming from one of the rooms with its door ajar. Dorrie! The baby and her nanny were already there. For a moment Alexa's pulse leaped as she realized how close the baby was.

She was aware that Damas was watching her with thinly veiled disdain as she continued to follow the bellhop without veering toward the baby's room. With a sinking feeling she realized that she should have inquired about the baby at the desk. From Damas's glare she knew that she had given the impression that the baby's whereabouts were of little concern. Mia would have rushed in to see why Dorrie was crying, but Alexa couldn't. She had to avoid the nanny at all costs. Clara was the one person who might notice little subtleties that would give the impersonation away.

Damas stopped at one of the smaller doors closest to the elevator and inserted his key. "Well, I guess I'm not right next door," he admitted with a grin. "But close enough, I'd say. Under different circumstances, the arrangement might be quite cozy, wouldn't you say?"

He was taunting her with the disappointment he thought she must be feeling because Guy wasn't going to be using that room. Mia and her lover would have had a nice setup. The accommodations would have been perfect for the few days together before Mia's husband arrived. The lovers couldn't have asked for a better arrangement, but the same heavenly situation added up to a horror for Alexa. Damas had read her expression correctly—she was disappointed, all right, but not for the reason he thought.

The doorman unlocked the double doors and waited for her to precede him into the suite. Her eyes widened and a gasp almost reached her lips as she stepped into utter luxury that belonged in television's "Lifestyles of the Rich and Famous."

The living room floated in air, with white walls and soft cloudlike carpet. Danish-Modern chairs and sofas were covered in sky blue damask, with accents in spring green tones. A white grand piano flanked by huge pots of greenery and fresh flowers dominated one end of the room, while at the opposite end, there was a modernistic fireplace faced with white brick. The suite included two spacious bedrooms, each with a marble bath and Jacuzzi, also a dining or conference room large enough to seat a dozen people and a pantry kitchen for catering.

As the bellman showed her through the rooms, Alexa felt like someone who had bought a ticket to tour the luxurious accommodations. She couldn't believe that she was expected to take such opulence for granted.

Some of the luggage had already been brought up and waited in the largest bedroom. Alexa viewed the mound of expensive bags with disbelief. Mia must spend a fortune on clothes. Alexa was used to keeping within a tight budget, buying items that could be worn more than one season. She always shopped sales and never gave in to impulse buying. Every unexpected expenditure that made a dent in Alexa's modest teaching salary was cause for worry. Mia must change clothes several times a day to have a need for all the outfits packed in those suitcases, thought Alexa, stunned once more by the differences in their lifestyles.

"Two maids have been assigned to this suite for your personal attention," the bellman told her. "Just press the blue button on the phone when you want their services."

Alexa suddenly felt sick. Trying to take in the opulence that surrounded her was like eating too much rich food.

"We want your stay at Foxfire to be perfect in every way, Mrs. Santini," the bellman recited in a mechanical way. "Whatever we can do, let us know."

Please, help me get away from here!

For one horrible moment, Alexa was panicked that she had spoken the plea aloud, but the bellman's expression remained placid. When he gave her a practiced smile and just stood there, she realized that he was waiting for a tip. She reached into Mia's purse and fingered the one-dollar bill and the five-dollar bill. Cowered by his officious manner, she reluctantly gave him the five dollars. How was she going to manage with only one wrinkled dollar bill in an expensive alligator purse that wasn't hers?

The bellman went out and closed the door with a devastating finality. A chill that went bone-deep brought a shiver rippling up Alexa's spine. She was trapped in an elegant suite with two maids, a chauffeur, nanny and a bodyguard to watch her every move. The longer she continued the impersonation, the more dangerous it became.

She wanted to telephone Mia, tell her that the situation was impossible, explain that she'd never be able to slip away with the baby and urge her to find another safe place before Leo learned of their relationship.

Yet her sister's vow haunted her. Alexa couldn't trust what Mia would do. If she called and told Mia the plan was off, her sister might harm herself before Alexa could get home. She remembered how chilling her twin's voice had been. *How can I give up without at least trying?* She began to pace the sitting room. She always thought better on her feet and gave most of her lectures that way.

All right, what to do next? For the moment she was Mia Santini, vacationing in luxurious surroundings that would have put Alexa in hock for ten years. What would her sister do first?

Go see the baby.

Warmth drained from her cheeks, but she knew that her only hope for success was to act as if she were Mia. If she didn't, someone like Clara was bound to speculate on the reason. Alexa straightened her shoulders and moistened her dry lips. She didn't have to be friendly or chatty with the nanny, she reminded herself. She'd give her attention to Dorrie and see how she might manage to get the baby away without suspicion.

Alexa opened the door of the suite and waited a minute before stepping out. She was surprised to see that the door to the room Damas had taken was closed. Maybe he wasn't going to monitor her every move after all. Hope like a geyser gushed through her.

The sounds of a television were still coming through the half-open door to the suite where she'd heard the baby crying. Without knocking or announcing her presence, she walked into a sitting room flanked by two bedrooms. The furnishings were chic and modern, but not as luxurious as the main suite.

Alexa ignored the bedroom where the television was blaring and peeked in the door of the other room. The baby was in the middle of a double bed, on her stomach, wiggling toward the edge. Alexa gave a cry, bounded across the room, but she was too late. Before she could reach the bed, Dorrie tumbled off and landed on her forehead with a thud that seemed to Alexa loud enough to break her tiny skull.

Alexa gathered the shrieking baby up in her arms just as Damas came through the door at a run.

"What happened?"

"She fell off the bed. Hit her forehead...."

"Let me see." He put his broad hands on each side of the baby's head, holding it steady while he examined her. He nodded. "Looks like she'll have a goose egg, all right."

"What'll we do?"

"Ice." He left the room and was back in quick time with a couple of ice cubes wrapped in a washcloth. "Here, let me have her."

Damas took Dorrie, sat down on the bed and bounced her slightly as he applied a cloth with ice cubes to her forehead. He sent Alexa a reassuring smile. "Don't look so worried, Mrs. Santini. Babies take falls all the time. They're tougher than they seem."

"How do you know?" Worry made her tone sound uncharitable.

"I was the eldest in a family of eight kids. Did plenty of baby-sitting. Bruised knees and bumps are my specialty."

His light tone helped. Dorrie was already quieting down. Alexa was beginning to breathe more normally. "Shouldn't we call a doctor?"

"She's all right. Aren't you, honey?"

He removed the ice and Dorrie's smoky blue eyes were suddenly dry. In spite of herself Alexa was grateful he had taken over. The antagonism between them was put aside for the moment. She gazed about the room. A lot of baby paraphernalia was scattered around, but there was no baby's crib or high chair.

"Where's the nanny?" Damas asked.

"I can make a guess." Alexa indicated the other bedroom. "The television's so loud she didn't even hear the baby fall." The more Dorrie had cried, the angrier Alexa had become. What kind of a nurse-maid would go off and leave a baby alone on a bed? Surely she could have heard the baby screaming. Why hadn't she come?

"The woman should be fired" Alexa's anger over the baby's fall suddenly spawned the answer to her dilemma. Could she really get away with firing Clara? *Why not? You're Mrs. Santini, the mother of the baby. You have every right to dismiss the woman for incompetence.* With the nanny gone, she could take charge of the baby and be ready to seize the first opportunity to leave Foxfire.

Before her courage could fail her, Alexa marched across the sitting room and into the other bedroom. The sight that met her eyes fueled her anger even more. The woman was sprawled in a chair in front of the television set, obviously in a deep sleep. Her head was thrown back, her mouth hung open and there was an empty bottle of beer on the floor beside the chair.

Alexa forgot to be cautious. Her reaction to the baby's fall and the nanny's incompetence was pure Alexa Widmire. She didn't even stop to think how her sister would have handled the incident. Inept people infuriated her, especially those who abused their authority. She kicked the woman's foot none too gently. "Wake up!"

The woman sat up with a start. "Oh, dear, I must have dropped off for a minute. The trip and all. The baby was fussy. Nothing was ready...."

"So you left Dorrie unattended—"

"She was asleep and I... I just thought I'd watch a bit of TV before she woke up."

"You're not paid to watch television, drink beer and sleep. Dorrie fell off the bed and even her screams didn't wake you up."

Clara's eyes fled to Damas standing in the doorway, holding the baby. Dorrie's cheeks were still tear streaked and an ugly bump was rising on her forehead, but she had quieted down.

"Oh, dear...."

"You're dismissed," snapped Alexa. "Please collect your things." She spoke in the same firm and authoritative tone she would have used to expel a student from her class.

Damas's eyes narrowed and he searched her face as if her decisive action had surprised him. She faltered for a moment, wondering if she had betrayed herself. Now that she thought about it, she had no idea how Mia would have handled the situation. Once again she was painfully aware of how little she knew about her sister.

Clara was protesting, but Alexa ignored her. She turned to Damas. "Will you arrange for the driver to take her back to the city? And have someone bring all the baby's things into my suite."

She took the baby from him. "I'll be keeping her with me from now on."

She closed her ears to Clara's tirade and walked back to the suite. Closing the door, she leaned weakly against it and shut her eyes for a second. Tiny fingers grabbed her nose and gave it a pull.

Startled, Alexa laughed and playfully kissed away the warm little hand. She hugged the baby and a swell of emotion brought warm tears dribbling down Alexa's cheeks. The beautiful baby girl in her arms mysteriously tapped feelings she had never known before.

"It's okay, honey. Auntie's going to take you home to Mommy."

Chapter Six

Damas only half listened to Clara's ranting as he stood in the doorway and watched Alexa disappear into the suite with the baby. Mia Santini's incongruous behavior puzzled him. Her anxiety and fury over the baby's fall had turned her into a mother lion. And yet, upon their arrival at the hotel, she hadn't asked about her daughter. She'd shown no interest when they'd stepped out of the elevator and heard the baby crying. A conscientious mother would have gone to see what was the matter, but she had gone on to her suite as if unconcerned. And yet when the baby had fallen off the bed, she'd been so distraught she hadn't known what to do. Her anxiety had quickly turned to anger and she had fired the nanny with a professional hauteur. For the first time, he wondered if Leo's wife had everybody fooled. Maybe she wasn't as shallow and narcissistic as her reputation indicated. He had a reliable intuition that vibrated like an antenna when someone was trying to checkmate him. The instinct had kept him alive more than once. Behind her self-centered facade, he had glimpsed a cunning intelligence that might make a fool out of any man if he was caught off guard. He smiled. Maybe this job would turn out to be interesting after all. *I think I've got your number, baby.*

"Simmer down, Clara. Mrs. Santini was just letting off a little steam. Her husband does the hiring and firing and she knows it. But she has the right to blow up when somebody's not doing her job."

"Tain't my fault the crib wasn't delivered before we got here," the fat woman snapped. "The baby was sound asleep when I put her down. I just dropped off for a minute—"

"A minute is all it takes with kids. You're damn lucky she wasn't hurt. Leo would peel your skin in a way that wouldn't be nice at all."

"Leo would never hurt me! We're family."

Damas snorted. "He'd throw his own mother in a cement mixer if it suited him and you know it."

"I'll tell him you said that," she threatened.

"You do that. We could have a nice little chat about you boozing on the job. Now, call housekeeping and see what's holding up things for the nursery."

"I don't take orders from you... or Mrs. Santini, either. I have a notion to phone Leo and tell him what happened. He'll blow for sure when he finds out she tried to fire me. I've never seen her look like that before. She didn't seem like herself at all."

"Just give her a little time to cool off."

Clara snorted. "She don't scare me none. Acting all uppity. Telling me I was fired! Wait till Leo gets here. He'll settle her down fast enough."

She was still ranting when Damas walked out on her and settled himself in the lounge area. No one could get to the elevator without passing him.

INSIDE THE SUITE, Alexa's emotions were on a yo-yo. Getting rid of the nanny was a big relief. Now she didn't have to worry about Clara sensing something was different about her. Damas was sprawled in an easy chair outside, looking insufferably relaxed and innocent. No chance to bolt from the suite with the baby.

Patience, she told herself. *One step at a time.* She didn't know what to do with Dorrie now that she had her all to herself. Babies were on schedules to eat and sleep, but that was about all she knew. She'd been raised a single child in an adult world. She had never experienced the sense of spontaneous love and affection she did at that moment, holding the gurgling baby in her arms. A quiver of joy went through her. She had found her true family in her sister and niece.

Sitting down on the floor with Dorrie, she searched in Mia's purse for something for the baby to play with. In addition to the cosmetic bag, wallet and car keys, she found a small bottle of pills. "To be taken at bedtime," the label said. No wonder Mia had trouble sleeping, thought Alexa. Her life seemed to be one long hassle. Thank heavens Mia didn't have the pills. She could have used them to carry out her threat.

Alexa jiggled the keys and Dorrie watched them with wide eyes and drooling smile. Her little hands reached out for them, but her eye-hand coordination needed a lot of practice, and Alexa laughed at her babyish effort to pull the keys to her mouth. Alexa couldn't believe the way things had worked out so beautifully. The nanny was out of the way and she had possession of Dorrie. The only obstacle left was Damas. She had to admit that when Dorrie tumbled off the bed, his presence had been reassuring. In truth, she had been startled by his deft handling of the baby. For a few moments he hadn't been his sarcastic, obnoxious self, and his telling her about his background had really surprised her. Not that she'd trust him to show that personable side to her again. She'd have to get by his guard somehow.

Holding Dorrie on her lap, she reached up, took the telephone off a small table and dialed her apartment.

Mia answered with a nervous "Hello?"

"Mia, it's me. I've got the baby."

"Thank heavens," Mia said in a choked sob. "Where are you?"

"Still at the resort."

"Why? Why don't you leave?" Her voice trembled impatiently. "You're taking too long."

Alexa pulled in a deep breath to halt a sharp reply. Mia seemed to think leaving was a matter of walking out the front door and hailing a cab. "There's a problem—"

"I want my baby. I'm going out of my mind with worry. Please hurry," Mia pleaded. "Come back *now.*"

"It's not that simple, Mia." She decided against letting her sister know that she'd fired Clara. Mia was already worried enough. Telling her about the fall and the ugly bump on Dorrie's head would only send her into a panic.

Either Alexa's hesitation or some sixth sense caused Mia to ask anxiously, "Dorrie...are you sure she's all right?"

"She's fine, sitting on my lap...slobbering over your car keys." Dorrie giggled as if she knew she was the subject of conversation. The baby's happy, sparkling face made Alexa smile. "She's such a darling, Mia."

"I miss her so. Please bring her to me."

"I will. Just as soon as I can. Is Mrs. Trimble taking care of you?"

"She wrapped my ankle and brought me some lunch."

"Good. Now, you just try to relax. I have the baby... I'll get away as soon as I can."

"If everyone thinks you're me, why can't you just walk out of the hotel with the baby and take a cab back?"

"Because the fellow taking Guy's place isn't about to let that happen. Your husband wants his wife at Foxfire when he arrives next week and this blasted new bodyguard isn't going to let me get a foot away from the place. I think Santini has given strict orders not to let you leave before he gets here."

"I've been such a fool. Why did I ever let myself get involved with Guy? I'm so worried. Have you heard anything about him?"

"No. And I didn't think it wise to ask. I've got my hands full with his replacement. I can't make a move without this fellow breathing down my neck. I'm afraid he's onto me."

"You mean he knows you're not me?"

"No. I mean he's wise to my trying to get away. He probably thinks that I...I mean *you*...don't want to be here when your husband arrives. I'm sure he knows I'm trying to give him the slip, and he isn't about to let that happen. I'm afraid that he doesn't think much of you. It's easy to see he's resentful that your husband put him on this job. It must be a comedown from what he's been doing, but he's not about to slack off. He's about as insufferable as they come."

"He must be a real goon."

Goon? Alexa thought about Damas's dark, arresting eyes, the molded firmness of cheeks and chin and the body that was coordinated and gracefully muscular. "No, he's...he's not the usual strong-arm type. He's domineering enough, but..." She remembered the way his large hands had curled tenderly around Dorrie as he'd soothed her.

"What does he look like?"

"Oh, I suppose some women might find him ruggedly attractive," Alexa conceded. And then she remembered how his smile was always taunting her. "If you like a dominating, conceited male, he fits the bill. I've come close to raking my nails across his face a couple of times. It's going to give me great pleasure to put his neck in a noose with your husband when I...you...show up missing."

"He sounds awful. Not like Guy. He was always so understanding and tender—" Mia's voice broke. "He always took such good care of me."

Alexa swallowed back a swearword. The whole blasted mess was due to the "good care" he had given her sister. As for Leo Santini, he sounded about as warm as an arctic iceberg. She could understand how her sister had foolishly taken a lover to fill the void, but in any case, it was too late for recriminations. "Don't cry, Mia. It's going to be all right. You'll have your baby soon and that will make everything fine."

"Are you sure you can get away?"

"I'm sure," Alexa replied in a confident tone. "I'll keep the baby here with me and as soon as I can give my watchdog the slip, I'll be on my way back with Dorrie."

"Tonight?"

Alexa hesitated. No use building up her sister's expectations. "I can't say. Just sit tight."

"Give Dorrie a kiss for me."

Alexa hung up and did as she was asked. "This is from your mommy." She buried her face in the baby's soft neck and snuggled her until Dorrie squealed.

A knock at the door spoiled the warm moment. Alexa froze. Then she stood up, clutching the baby in her arms. It was probably just a maid, she told herself. Someone bringing the baby crib and the rest of the paraphernalia.

But she was mistaken. When Alexa opened the door, Clara stood there. Her double chins quivered and her forehead furrowed in a scowl. "I've come for the baby."

Alexa was too dumbfounded to speak. The audacity of the woman was beyond belief. Before she could summon a vitriolic reply, Damas appeared behind Clara.

"May we come in?" he asked politely, as if she had a choice, but they didn't wait for an answer. He closed the door firmly behind them.

She had fired Clara. What was she doing here? Alexa took a step backward, feeling cornered and strangely off balance. And why was Damas looking at her as if she had been behaving stupidly? And then she knew. *I've done something terribly out of character.* Something Mia never would have done. Of course!

With frightening hindsight, Alexa realized her mistake. Mia didn't have the authority to dismiss staff— especially someone like Clara, who was related to Leo. *I should have known better,* Alexa admonished herself. She could feel the color draining from her face.

Damas was watching her closely. "I explained to Clara that you were upset—"

"But that don't give her any right to be treating me that way," Clara lashed out. "Ordering me to leave like some paid servant instead of family! Putting on airs." Her black eyes snapped. "Why you acting so funny, Mia?"

"I . . . I . . ." stammered Alexa. She floundered under the woman's piercing gaze. All the things she wanted to say to the obnoxious nanny were pure Alexa Widmire. Her sister's behavior was too alien. In a similar situation Mia would probably cry and apologize, but Alexa couldn't. She was adrift in an impersonation that demanded a response that was contrary to her nature. She tried to mask the conflict going on within her, but her expression must have given her turmoil away.

"You're not yourself, Mia." Clara's pudgy eyelids narrowed slightly and her mouth pursed. "Not at all."

Alexa sat down wearily on the sofa, still holding the baby in her arms. Time to end the masquerade. Time to try to defuse the deception as much as possible. *I'm sorry, Mia. I'm sorry.* She cleared her throat, not knowing how to begin.

"I told Clara that you've had several disappointments today," Damas said, watching her closely.

"I can see that she's in a muddle about something," granted Clara with her habitual snort. She pointed a thick finger at Alexa. "You get off your high horse, or I'll be on the phone to Leo. He'll straighten you out quick enough. Firing me! He put the baby in my charge the first day she came home from the hospital. You better be believing that I'll be tending her till the day she walks out of the house on her wedding day." She glared at Mia. "It's you who should be remembering her place, I'm thinking. It's the men in this family who run things."

Alexa's arms instinctively tightened around the baby, hugging her to her chest. Dorrie chortled as her little fingers tugged on a dangling strand of hair that had drifted forward on Alexa's cheek. She gave Alexa a wide, toothless smile that brought a flood of emotion surging through her with the force of a tidal wave. *I can't give her up. I can't!*

"Hand me the baby. It's time for her bottle."

Alexa touched her lips to Dorrie's soft head. What was she going to do? She couldn't just abandon the infant. Not with the child's future at stake. An emotional bonding between her and the baby made retreat impossible. But how could she stumble her way through the unfamiliar maze of being Mia without someone tumbling to the impersonation? Damas came up behind her and touched her shoulder.

"Why don't you check out the nursery? Make sure everything's the way you want it, Mia?"

He'd never used her first name before. Hearing it from his lips startled her for a moment, then gave her the spurt of confidence she needed. He still thought she was Mia. She hadn't given anything away. Thank heavens, she hadn't blurted out the truth. All she needed was a little more time. From now on she'd be more careful and do a better job of acting the part, until the next opportunity to get the baby presented itself.

"Yes," she said as she got to her feet, still holding the baby and ignoring Clara's movement to take her. "I'll carry Dorrie back."

Clara mumbled audibly all the way to the other suite. She stood by the crib as Alexa lowered the baby into it and handed her a rattle. But Dorrie wasn't ready to be put down, and let out a howl of protest.

Clara brushed Alexa aside with a broad hip. "I told you it was time for a bottle."

Alexa fought an urge to return the shove. She was aware of Damas leaning up against the door frame, watching.

Clara picked up the baby and glared at Mia as she fished in a diaper bag. "You go ahead and find a party like you always do. Get all dressed up and enjoy yourself. And don't be coming in here, waking the baby up at all hours, giving her one of your drunken good-night kisses."

The insight into Mia's behavior sent a shock through Alexa. *Find a party. Dress up and enjoy yourself. Drunken good-night kisses.* That was the pattern she had to follow if she wanted to continue the deception. She didn't look at Damas as he stepped back and let her walk past him.

He followed her out into the lounge area. "I warned Clara that she'd better watch her step or I'd tell Leo about the baby's fall."

Alexa nodded. She didn't know what the proper reply would be. The idea that only the males surrounding Mia had any power revolted her. She supposed that she should act eternally grateful to Damas for the support he seemed to be giving her. She wondered if Guy Lentz had wheedled his way into Mia's heart by doing the same thing. The image she was getting of her sister's life sickened her.

She stopped at the door of her suite. "I'm going to take a shower and rest." *If that meets with your approval,* she added under her breath.

"What are your plans for tonight, Mrs. Santini?"

She stiffened. So he was back to being formal. No "Mia" this time, no trace of the reassuring tone he had used a moment earlier. He must have recognized the unspoken hostility in her brisk tone. She'd have to be more careful.

"Why do you ask?"

"I was just wondering when you'd be going downstairs."

Not *if* but *when.* A hard knot settled in Alexa's chest. He expected her to follow Mia's social whirl. How could she get out of it? Pretend she was ill? That would mean she'd be trapped in her room with him parked like a sentry outside her door. She'd have a better chance of slipping away if she moved around the hotel.

She gave him what she hoped was a neutral smile. "About eight."

Without waiting for his comment, she went into her suite and shut the door. She leaned back against it and closed her eyes. The last thing she felt like doing was carrying this horrible charade into the midnight hours.

Chapter Seven

When she emerged from the suite at fifteen minutes
past eight, Damas was waiting for her. His eyes swept
over her elaborate hairstyle, jewels and designer gown,
and Alexa was confident that she was Mia Santini
from head to toe.

As Damas stepped into the elevator with Alexa, an
unsettling seductive perfume touched his nostrils. He
was poignantly aware of her utter femininity as she
stood beside him. She wore a gown made of a white
clinging material and her sweet neck showed soft and
smooth above a low-cut neckline. A hint of cleavage
and caressable full breasts held his gaze a moment
longer than he would have liked. The skirt of the gown
fell to a uneven hemline and swirled around her like
giant sheer handkerchiefs draped to show her supple
legs and silver slippers. He found himself suddenly
growing very warm.

She gave him the hint of a knowing smile. Her eyes
sparkled like the diamond drops in her ears, as if she
were enjoying some undefinable success. Damn the
woman. She was as changeable as a chameleon. He
had almost liked her when she had been so distraught

about the baby. The way she had clung to the infant had touched a soft spot. Trying to stand up to Clara, she seemed terribly vulnerable and innocent. He'd been surprised at himself—he'd felt a compulsion to protect her. Even fight her battles. Despite all his experiences with women, he was still a sucker for a gal who was trying to lick the odds. And Mia Santini had a stacked deck against her. But there was nothing innocent and helpless about the way she looked tonight. She had learned to use the weapon she had—her desirable, utterly womanly body. Her feminine charms were a baited hook and there were bound to be suckers who would be blinded by the glittering lure. *But not me, sweetheart. Not me.*

"You look very nice tonight, Mrs. Santini," he said in a mocking tone.

"Thank you."

There was a satisfied curve to her ruby red lips. Her measuring eyes took in his white pants, dress shirt and navy blue jacket. He'd chosen a silk maroon tie, held in place by a gold clip; matching cuff links glittered in snowy white cuffs. He had to silently laugh at her expression. She raised an eyebrow as if surprised that he would be indistinguishable from any of the guests. He wondered how Guy Lentz had dressed. Undoubtedly she was wishing it were her lover standing close enough to breathe her perfume and put a hand on the curve of her waist. What a disappointment. No wonder she resented him. *Too bad, lady. You're stuck with me.*

As if to make it clear that she didn't consider him an escort, she stepped out of the elevator without waiting for him and headed across the lobby, not acknowledging his presence at all. As he followed casually behind her, he could have been a complete stranger for all the notice she gave him.

He watched her survey the lobby, hesitate for a moment as she glanced out the front door, and then she turned and headed for the lounge. It figured, he thought wryly. What better place to find herself some new partying friends? She wouldn't have to buy a single drink if his guess was right. She was something to look at all right. Her hips swung gracefully in rhythm with the long legs showing in the openings of the handkerchief skirt. Her shiny hair floated around her face like spun gold. She was elegantly dressed, perfumed and ready for unwrapping. A lady out on the town. He frowned. Something was wrong. Out of focus. What was it? What was nagging at him?

He watched her pause in the doorway of the dimly lighted lounge, not like a beautiful woman about to make an entrance, but like someone taking a deep breath to steel her courage. He saw her hands clench nervously at her sides. She didn't radiate the relaxed air of a rich woman ready for a good time. Her back was too straight. He could see the rapid rise and fall of her breath. *What in blazes was going on?* Why was Mia Santini acting scared to death, like some schoolgirl dressed up for her first party?

ALEXA TOOK a seat at the bar, not knowing if that was the right thing to do. Maybe she should ask for a table or join one of the laughing groups clustered around the room. She had a whole evening ahead to play the party girl, and at the moment, she didn't have a clue how to begin.

"Good evening. What's your pleasure?" The bartender's mouth parted in a white-toothed smile under a precisely manicured thin mustache.

"Gin and tonic." She had decided that would be a safe drink for a long evening. In a crowd no one would notice when she changed to water. She would play her part well, because her best chance of getting away with the baby sometime during the night was to convince Damas that she'd had too much to drink and pretend to be on the verge of passing out when he followed her back to the suite.

A roar of laughter behind her got her attention and she locked eyes with a tall man with gray sideburns, who obviously had been staring at her. He wore formal evening clothes and sat between two dark-haired young women who were leaning suggestively in his direction. Instinctively Alexa looked away and turned back to her drink. *I can't do it.*

The bartender set down her drink. He didn't seem to expect payment. Probably all the hotel guests ran a tab.

"Pardon me...but aren't you Mia Santini?"

The man who had been staring at her had left his table and now stood beside her stool. His face was nicely tanned, his fortyish body well preserved and his hair jet black except for the gray sideburns, which gave him a refined look.

Alexa slowly took a sip of her drink and looked over the rim of her glass at him. *The point of no return.* She lowered the glass. "Who wants to know?"

"Zurick...Frank Zurick. Our paths have crossed, but I've never had the opportunity to introduce myself. I'm surprised to find you alone." His smile was openly flirtatious. "A beautiful woman like you should always be surrounded by admirers. Would you do me the honor of joining my party?"

Alexa languidly set her glass down on the bar, while her thoughts raced. The last thing she wanted was a dialogue with someone who was trying to make time with Mia. But the alternative of sitting by herself was worse. At least this fellow looked intelligent.

She turned around on the stool and looked at the people seated at his table. She frowned as if deciding whether the company was pleasing. "Do I know anybody?"

"Probably not. Just friends and acquaintances of mine. Not from the New York scene. Come on. I'll introduce you."

"All right." She gave him a vague smile as she slid off the stool and he put a guiding hand on her arm. His fingers deliberately played along her bare skin as he maneuvered her around chairs and tables. *Where was Damas?* She didn't see him anywhere. Her irritation was unreasonable and she knew it. He was just following her lead. Her manner had told him plainly enough to get lost. Why on earth was she thinking of him in terms of protection? He was the biggest threat she faced. If she stubbed her toe pretending to be Mia, he'd be the first to bring the impersonation crashing down upon her head.

"I've persuaded Mia to join us," Zurick said smoothly, somehow managing to pull up a chair for her, which forced one of the brunette beauties to move farther around the table.

He introduced everyone, but the five names that

rolled off his tongue were lost on Alexa except one . . . Rhonda from D.C. She was not pleased with the addition to the party. From her glare, Alexa sensed the woman was sharpening her darts even before she sat down. Zurick held up a manicured finger and signaled the barmaid.

Alexa ordered another gin and tonic, even though her first one sat half-full on the bar. A florid-faced man with a shiny bald head launched into some story that brought the level of laughter at the table back to the decibel it had been before Alexa had joined the group.

She gratefully let the conversation and laughter whirl around her. Zurick leaned back in his chair, letting his gaze boldly settle on Alexa as he drank his Scotch. Rhonda bristled, then finished off her martini and ordered another one.

"Where's your husband, Mia?" Rhonda's smile had all the charm of a snake rattle. "Are we going to have the honor of meeting the notorious Leo Santini? Is he here with you?"

"No."

"He's a well-known figure in D.C., you know. The papers are always full of his . . . enterprises." She gave a brittle laugh. "He certainly keeps a step ahead of the law, doesn't he?"

"Careful, Rhonda. The walls have ears, you know," the bald man cautioned with a nervous glance at Alexa.

"I don't give a—"

"Rhonda, I think you should take a trip to the powder room, don't you?" Zurick interrupted smoothly as he set down his glass. A gold-and-diamond ring glistened on his little finger as he touched Alexa's arm with his soft hand. "Mia, will you join me for dinner?"

Join *me?* Not *us?* What should she do? The way Rhonda was going after her, she might be better off dining alone with Zurick. She glanced at her watch. Almost nine o'clock. She should be able to parlay dinner into a two-hour affair. That should be enough time to convince Damas that she was consumed with drink and food and ready to give in to sleep for the night.

She threw Zurick what she hoped was a coquettish smile. "Yes, thank you. I'm quite hungry all of a sudden." She hoped her smile hid the bald-faced lie. Her nervous stomach was warning her that it wasn't going to tolerate an intake of rich food. Even though she had sipped only half of two drinks, she could feel the gin sending a light feeling to her head.

As Zurick guided her out of the lounge into the lobby, she glanced around and still didn't see Damas. She couldn't decide whether she was relieved or annoyed. What if she was going through this elaborate eating-and-drinking charade for nothing? Maybe he had taken himself off somewhere.

"Are you looking for someone," Zurick asked.

"Not really," Alexa lied. "Just seeing who's here."

"You're not going to desert me for another dinner partner, are you? Several times when I had glimpses of you at some function, I looked forward to the day fate would throw us together." His fingertips moved slightly on her arm in a suggestive caress. "Do you believe in fate, Mia?" he asked smoothly, as if uttering a well-worn line.

Somehow she managed a vague smile. "I don't know...do you?"

At that moment, she caught a glimpse of Damas through some greenery in a glass brick planter. She couldn't tell whether he had followed them out of the lounge or had been waiting in the lobby. He didn't look at her as he ambled toward the dining room, keeping a measured distance between them. She moved away from Zurick's possessive touch, even as she chided herself for caring what Damas might think.

"Mrs. Santini." The officious bellman overtook them just as they reached the dining room door. "There's a call waiting for you. From your husband."

Alexa's stomach dipped as if the floor had suddenly dropped out from under her. *Leo! On the phone!* The possibility that he'd call had never crossed her mind. How could she know what to say to him? A married couple's intimate relationship was between only them. She had never seen Mia and Leo together. She had no idea how her sister behaved or responded to her husband. *And what about Guy?* What should she do or say if Santini accused her of unfaithfulness?

"I can bring a phone to your table, if you like," offered the bellman when Alexa failed to respond.

"No, that won't be necessary." She swallowed against a dry mouth. "Why don't you go ahead and get us a table?" she said to Zurick. "And I'll join you in a few minutes."

Zurick nodded formally. "Of course."

"I'll take the call in my room," she told the bellman, and brushed past him. She walked quickly back to the lobby, not sure whether she should ignore the waiting call or try to bluff her way through it. Thank heavens her voice and Mia's were as identical as their looks. But Santini was a smart man. He'd kept a step ahead of the law; a man in his position didn't trust anyone. Anything out of the ordinary would surely alert his attention. What should she do? At best, she had only a few hours to try to make her escape with the baby.

In her sudden turmoil, she'd forgotten about Damas, but before she reached the elevator, he fell in step beside her.

"You blasted little fool!" he growled. "What in the hell are you trying to do...get yourself killed and half of Chicago laid out on a slab?"

She was too flabbergasted to answer. His fury was like a clap of thunder. He ushered her past the elevator and, keeping a firm grip on her, led her out a terrace door. A night breeze carrying the scent of pine touched her flushed face. Beyond a landscaped garden, the lake shimmered silver in the moonlight. He guided her past several couples who were on the terrace, enjoying the view. They had taken a few steps along a garden path, when she collected herself and jerked away from him. Her tone was not Mia Santini's, but her own. "Just what do you think you're doing?"

"Trying to save that pretty neck of yours." His mouth twisted unpleasantly. "That's what I'm paid to do, isn't it? Of all the weak-brained, stupid women I've ever met, you take the prize, Mia Santini."

Why was he lashing out at her with clenched jaw and flashing eyes? She hadn't the foggiest idea what she'd done to make him so furious. She'd just been doing what Clara had said Mia usually did. *Dress up and find herself a party.* "I don't know what you're talking about."

"I'm talking about Frank Zurick. Don't play innocent with me. You know damn well who he is."

"No, I—"

"Come off it! Zurick's been feuding with your husband for years. As head of the Chicago syndicate, he's been trying to move in on the New York scene. He wants Leo out of power one way or another. And you're playing right into his hands."

Zurick! A Chicago gangster!

Damas must have taken her silence for admission. "How do think it looks, you flirting with your husband's worst enemy? If Zurick gets you in any kind of a compromising situation, they'll be more blood on the streets than in any Chicago slaughterhouse."

She couldn't find her voice to say anything. He was talking about a world she had seen only in movies…where the good guys always won. But this wasn't make-believe and in real life mobsters like Leo Santini— She put a hand up to her mouth and gasped. "The phone. Leo's on the phone."

Damas's laugh was short. "Relax, Mia. Your husband didn't call. I set up the phone call to get you away from Zurick."

Alexa's anger swelled for a brief moment before it dissipated in relief. Because of Damas's interference, she'd been spared a perilous contact with Mia's husband. A narrow escape. One thing was glaringly clear—she had to get away before a real call came through. Next time she might not be so lucky.

She caught Damas registering the surge of emotion that must have been evident on her face. He startled her by saying, "It's a damn good thing Leo wasn't calling you, Mia."

The remark matched her thoughts too closely. But he had called her "Mia." She didn't trust herself to speak.

"All hell would have broken loose if you'd told him you were about to have dinner with Zurick. I can't imagine your being so stupid. Both our necks could be in a noose. Why would you pick up with a guy like that? He was only using you to get to Leo."

She turned abruptly away. How could she discuss anything with him, when everything she said would be a lie? The urge to run was overwhelming. She ignored the sound of his following footsteps as she headed down the garden path at a brisk gait. She needed time to organize her thoughts, look at the situation in some rational way and decide what to do next.

She was angry with herself for not being more careful. But how could she have known that she was being picked up by a Chicago mobster? Frank Zurick could have passed for a professor at Hunter College. How stupid she had been to think she could blithely step into Mia's shoes. She shivered just thinking about living day to day in such a world. Always confronted with violence. Insecurity. Manipulation. Constantly on guard against an innocent move that might spark retaliation between mob bosses. This had been Mia's life—and would become Dorrie's if she was raised in the same environment. *No, I can't let that happen.*

Alexa stopped at the edge of the lake, fighting a rising panic as she stood there. A quivering reflection of the moon rose and fell on the water and the wooded hills mounted dark against the night sky held a quiet beauty. She drew deep breaths of air into her tight chest. The quiet calm of the scene, the lapping and sucking rhythm of the water, soothed her raw-edged nerves. Taut muscles around her mouth eased and she unconsciously thrust her chin forward. There was still time. Yet nothing had changed. She still had to get past Damas's guard, one way or another.

Damas leaned up against the trunk of an oak tree, watching Alexa as she stood motionless at the water's edge. A teasing breeze playfully tugged at the soft clinging fabric of her white gown, molding her breasts and lifting the uneven hemline to show her long legs and silver slippers. Moonlight bathed her face and figure, and he was much too aware of the sweet slope of her bare shoulders and the tantalizing lift of her chin. He cursed himself for wanting to touch the delicate smoothness of her face, and feel the wondrous flowing line and curve of her body. His desire was more than just physical attraction. He couldn't define what mystique she held for him. He knew only that he was dangerously close to losing all perspective where Mia Santini was concerned.

He'd been around beautiful women before, plenty of them, but there was something different and intriguing about this one. She kept giving mixed signals. He thought he had her number because of her reputation—she was supposed to be a boozer, yet she'd left two half-finished drinks in the bar. He had watched her ill-at-ease manner at Zurick's table. She hadn't mixed easily or contributed anything to the conversation, and yet she let herself be picked up and acted surprised at finding out who Zurick was. What kind of game was she playing? He stuck his hand in his pocket and fingered the diamond earring. The cold metal and jewels were a good reality check. He remembered the tumbled bed and the lingering scent of her perfume at Guy's apartment. He straightened up, shoving aside a sudden anger that he refused to explain. He walked over to her. "Ready to go back in?"

"I guess I should send word back to Zurick," she said without looking at him.

"No need. When you don't come back, he'll get the message. Not that he'll give up. There's too much satisfaction in making your husband look the fool. He's probably already ordered flowers delivered to your suite."

She put a hand to her throat and turned away. As she started back toward the hotel, she wavered on the path. Damas caught up with her and offered his arm. After a moment's hesitation, she accepted it.

"Thank you. I feel a little . . . unsteady."

"You need food."

He felt a shudder go through her.

"I couldn't go back to the dining room."

"There's room service, I believe," he said sarcastically.

Her relieved expression was genuine. He didn't know whether all this was a ploy of some kind. He knew only that feeling her sweet length close to his side sent his male hormones firing like a booster rocket.

IN THE SHADOWS of the terrace, Malchek watched as they walked up the steps and into the hotel. He dropped his cigarette and stepped on it. The evening was still young, and the boss's wife had already given him plenty of goodies to report.

Leo would be real interested to know she'd been drinking with Zurick, walking in the moonlight with Silva. He'd bet Silva and she were headed to her suite now.

Chapter Eight

Damas left Alexa at her suite with a gruff "Good night."

She shut the door without responding. His "good night" was painfully ironic. The only thing that stood between her and a *good* night was Damas Silva. She wasn't going to give up on the plan to leave with the baby. Somehow, she had to find a way to get by him before morning.

She walked over to the wide expanse of windows. Below her, lights dotted the landscaped grounds and the lake shimmered like a dark blue jewel. A few minutes ago she and Damas had stood at the water's edge. She could make out the path they had walked on to the lake and back. His nearness had created a whirlwind of emotions. Every sense had been strangely heightened and his disturbing male essence had aroused a latent femininity she'd never experienced before. Feelings she had thought alien to her nature stirred in her—a longing to be touched, to be caressed and treasured. This sudden vulnerability was frightening.

Wearily she kicked off the silver slippers and sat down on the edge of the king-size bed. Her reflection in the vanity mirror mocked her utter failure as a social butterfly. She might look like a party girl, but underneath the soft, flowing gown and golden curls, she was Alexa Widmire. Pretending to think and act like Mia had only resulted in a pathetic fiasco.

Alexa shivered, thinking of the damage she might have already done by joining Zurick's table in the bar. What would the Chicago mobster do next? Being stood up for dinner wouldn't sit well with any man's pride. He was probably smarting from the callous way she had walked out on him. Damas had warned her that Zurick wouldn't give up trying to get her into a compromising situation. More than ever, Mia Santini needed to disappear. Alexa shivered. What should she do now?

She'd been on a roller coaster all day and lunch seemed like an eternity ago. She picked up the menu placed by the telephone and ordered an expensive meal that would have done her sister proud.

While she waited for the food to be delivered, she changed clothes. The white party dress went back on a hanger. Unable to find a pair of faded jeans and a baggy sweatshirt, she decided on ivory stirrup pants and a short-sleeved pullover decorated with pastel flowers.

When a steward delivered the serving cart, Alexa let him in and then peeked out the open door. She expected to see Damas sitting in the lounge area, strategically placed between the suite and the elevator, but was surprised to find that he was nowhere in sight. The door to his room was closed. Was this the chance she'd been waiting for? Her pulse began to race.

"Where would you like to be served?" asked the young man. He had a napkin draped over one arm and was waiting in the middle of the sitting room.

Served! Good heavens, he expected to remain with the food and wait on her. "Just leave the cart there. That'll be fine. I'll ring when I'm finished." She stood back and waited for him to leave.

He opened his mouth as if to protest and then just shrugged. "Sign here."

She scribbled Mia's name on the slip and hastily added a twenty-five percent tip.

"Thank you very much."

He gave her a broad smile as he left. She heard him whistling softly as he waited for the elevator.

Where were the stairs? Alexa cursed herself for not locating the fire exit earlier. She studied instructions and diagrams mounted on the back of the door. The only staircase was just beyond Damas's room. She'd have to pass it in order to get to the stairs, but maybe he wasn't in his room. Maybe he was down in the lobby, watching the elevator.

She forgot about food. This might be her only chance to get past him. If he was watching the elevator, she had a chance of making it down the stairs and out the building.

Grabbing a jacket and Mia's purse, she slipped out the door. Still no sign of Damas. The door to his room remained closed as she hurried across the open area. She eased open the door to the other suite and slipped inside. The ever-droning television sounded from Clara's room and Alexa prayed she was sleeping in front of it the way she had been in the afternoon. It would only take her a minute to get the baby and flee.

She made it to the door of the baby's room and then stopped short. In the radius of soft lamplight she saw Damas bending over the crib. *What was he going to do to the baby?* Fear lurched through her. She made a strangled gasp. He looked up and saw her standing in the doorway. He put a warning finger to his lips and motioned her out the bedroom ahead of him.

"What are you doing here?" Alexa demanded in a hushed tone. He'd checkmated her again.

He didn't answer her until he had guided her out the suite and shut the door. "Checking on the baby, what else? Just wanted to make sure Dorrie was where she ought to be." His knowing gaze slid over her jacket and change of clothes. "Planning on going out?"

He knew damn well what she'd been up to. He hadn't been watching her door because he'd guessed she wouldn't leave without the baby. She'd given herself away that afternoon when she'd clung to Dorrie and had harsh words with Clara. She knew exactly why he'd been in the baby's room. Staying close to Dorrie was as good as staying near her.

She bit her lip to keep from venting her disappointment and frustration. Her mind whirled. What now? This round went to him, but she wasn't down for the count. A natural stubbornness made her even more determined to outwit him. Maybe she had been approaching the whole thing wrong.

"I ordered a feast from room service," she told him as they reached her door. "Why don't you join me? That way both of us can...relax." There had to be a way to slip past his guard and she intended to find it before morning.

The invitation obviously startled him. One eyebrow raised slightly, as if he were amused by the unexpected challenge. Tiny smile lines darted away from his dark eyes. "Why, thank you, Mrs. Santini." He gave a slight mocking bow.

She wanted to slap his supercilious grin. His manner was deliberately insulting and she had to swallow back a sharp retort. As she preceded him into the suite, she allowed herself the satisfaction of saying curtly, "Leave the door open." She tossed the jacket and Mia's purse on the sofa.

"Yes, ma'am." His tone was pure derision. Sometimes she was as transparent as an eyeglass. As she walked across the room in tight pants that molded her rounded fanny, he wanted to turn her around and let her know that he wasn't falling for the sexy act. He wasn't a nice guy when some gal tried to sexually manipulate him.

He surveyed the suite, casually wandering over to each of the two bedroom doors, and peeked in the small denlike room off the sitting room. "Pretty nice," he said.

But she knew he hadn't been interested in the decor—more like "casing the joint," as the saying went. He stopped at the built-in bar and gazed at the unopened bottles of liquor.

Was he looking for evidence that she had been drinking? "Would you like a drink...or are you just taking an inventory?" she asked pointedly.

He peeked under the silver tureens on the service cart and nodded in approval. "Shrimp, scallops and lobster tails. Garden peas and salad with hollandaise sauce. Where's the white wine?''

"What?''

"Seafood demands white wine. You can't enjoy this kind of meal without it.''

I can—and do! she silently retorted. She'd ordered coffee to drink with the dinner, not wine. During the holidays or some special occasion she ordered wine, but she certainly had never thought a meal incomplete without it. *But you're not you. Mia would have ordered wine.* She knew she had unwittingly stepped out of character again.

"I did order some,'' she lied. She handed him the one large plate and took the smaller salad plate for herself. She hurriedly took a little of everything and then sat down on the sofa. "Help yourself.''

"Thanks.''

Once again his mouth curved with that derisive smile. He was just going to sit down on a chair opposite her, when a brisk knock sounded on the open door.

Alexa jumped and her heart took a sickening plunge.

"Shall I answer it?'' Damas asked.

She nodded.

A bellboy stood there with a huge bouquet of roses in his hands. "Flowers for Mia Santini.''

Damas took them and tipped the boy. He brought them back to Alexa. "One guess who they're from.'' A raw edge of anger deepened his voice. "I told you he wouldn't give up.''

A heavy floral scent filled Alexa's nostrils as she drew out the white card and pricked a finger on a sharp thorn. Drops of blood smeared the short message. "Until tomorrow. Frank."

A wave of weakness suddenly turned her body cold and trembling. There was a warning in the simple message. Inadvertently she had pitted two ruthless men against each other. One false step and she could be devoured by each of them.

She was vaguely aware of the flowers slipping from her lap onto the floor. The strong rose perfume was quickly suffocating. Her head fell back on the sofa cushion. A kaleidoscope of images formed behind her lids, wavering and reshaping themselves. *Mia's tearful face... Damas's profile... the baby's rosebud mouth... Zurick's calculating expression.* Her arms and legs floated away in an enveloping weakness. *Good Lord,* she thought, *I'm going to faint.*

"Here, drink this!" Damas cupped her face with one hand and held the glass to her lips with the other. She sputtered as fiery brandy slipped down her throat. Warmth rushed through her and Damas's face swam into focus. He was so close to her that she could feel the warmth of his breath on her cheek. On some detached level she was aware that his dark brown eyes were beautifully feathered with a touch of amber. She was almost mesmerized by the intensity of their shadowy depths, and it was a long moment before reality came rushing back and she pushed his hands away.

"Don't...don't," she stammered. He was sitting on the couch beside her. His mouth was much too close, his lips much too soft and sensuous. "Don't kiss me," she heard herself say, much to her horror.

His lips parted in a slow smile. "Are you trying to put ideas into my head, lady?"

"No, of course not. I just... I mean..." What did she mean? Why was she thinking about his seductive eyes and kissable mouth? He was looking at her with the gentleness she'd seen him show the baby. How easy it would be to forget he was Leo Santini's hired hand. Is this what had happened to Mia?

He reached in front of her.

"What are you doing?" She pulled back when his arm brushed against her breasts.

"Just getting your plate." He picked it up from the end table and handed it to her. "I don't want to deliver a sick wife to Leo when he gets here. Now, eat."

"I'm not hungry."

"Eat it by yourself... or I'll feed it to you." He stood up and looked down at her from his dominating height.

"You will not!"

"Try me." He waited.

She picked up a fork. She knew enough to back down. It wasn't easy, but she'd have to swallow her pride and concentrate on getting down some food.

He sat down opposite her, stretched his legs out in front of the chair in a relaxed manner. He eyed her from time to time to see how she was doing, as he cleaned his own plate.

Surprisingly enough after the first few bites, she began to relax and her stomach readily accepted the food. The nourishment did wonders for her. Her mind began to function again. There was still time to get out of this mess before morning. When Frank Zurick followed up on his "Until tomorrow" she'd be long gone. She knew what had to be done. Damas Silva had to be put out of commission. *You can do it,* she told herself as she set her empty plate aside.

He nodded. "That's better."

"Would you really have spoon-fed me?" she asked as he picked up both plates and set them on the cart. "Is that part of being a bodyguard?"

He shrugged. "I've never watched out for a woman before. I just know Leo wants his goods delivered on time and in good shape."

"Is that what I am . . . goods?"

"Aren't you?" His brazen look challenged her.

"I guess so," she admitted. "Just Leo's possessions. His wife. Dorrie. He owns everybody, doesn't he? Even you."

"Nobody owns me. And don't try needling me. It won't work. Whatever is going on between you and your husband has nothing to do with me or my feelings. Got that? I know my job. Don't expect me to swallow any poor-little-old-me baloney. You may have a lot of people fooled, but I'm not one of them. Under that fluff and tinsel you're plenty sharp. You knew what you were getting into when you got married. I just have one question. Why did you do a stupid thing like getting involved with Guy Lentz?"

"Maybe we fell in love."

"Love? What would we do without love to take the rap for such asinine behavior?"

"Have you ever been in love?"

"Sure. Lots of times. But I've never acted like some star-struck idiot. I don't know why women lose their heads when it comes to falling in love."

She thought a moment. "To a man, love is a thing apart, but to a woman, her whole existence."

He stared at her.

"I...read that somewhere," she said quickly, knowing that she had unwittingly dropped the mask she was trying to wear. Trying to cover up her fluster, she asked, "Shall we have coffee?"

"*Shall* we?" he mimicked, still studying her.

He was too sharp. *Mia never would have used "shall."* Alexa cursed her own stupidity. Every word out of her mouth brought her closer to disaster. Alluding to poetry...using precise English. She barely managed to keep her gaze steady as she returned his studied appraisal. "I'd like a cup of coffee... wouldn't you?"

He nodded thoughtfully as he rose from his chair and walked over to the serving cart. "Sugar? Cream?" he asked as he poured two cups.

"How about making it Irish coffee? Is there some whiskey on the bar?"

For a moment the corners of his mouth deepened, as if he were going to chide her about lacing the coffee with liquor. Then he seemed to change his mind. "A nightcap to help you sleep?"

"Yes...to help me relax."

As he turned away and walked the length of the room she quietly opened Mia's purse and eased out the bottle of pills. He had his back to her when she dropped three of them into one of the cups of coffee. Enough? Too many? She prayed the whiskey would cover up the sharp taste and reinforce the sedative.

He came back with a bottle of Wild Turkey. "We're in luck." He poured a generous shot into each cup. She reached for the coffee without the pills and sipped it approvingly. He took the other cup and sat back down in his chair.

She was too nervous to sit there and watch him drink the coffee. She had no idea how long it would take for the drug to take effect. "Will you excuse me a minute?" she asked with a false smile.

"Sure." He lazily assumed his relaxed position. She couldn't leave the suite without him seeing her pass his chair.

Alexa set down her cup with trembling hands. "Be back in a minute."

In the bathroom she stared into the mirror. She couldn't believe what she'd done. She detested dishonesty and deceit on any level. Integrity had always been important to her, and her students had respected her for it. She covered her face with her hands. In one day she had betrayed all her principles. What had trapped her into behaving contrary to the strict code of behavior she had always followed? The answer was simple. She couldn't give Mia and Dorrie up to some tyrannical mobster who would destroy their lives. No one had really ever needed her before. She'd found her very own family and the future of all three of them depended upon her.

She straightened up. Splashed water on her face. Glanced at her watch. Was it only eleven o'clock? It seemed like forever since she'd dressed up to go "partying." How long should she wait before seeing if Damas was asleep?

She moved quickly to the bedroom door and peered into the living room. He was sitting in the easy chair, his head back on the cushion and his eyes closed. Was

he asleep already? She strained to hear any sign of
heavy breathing as she moved farther into the room.

He didn't move. When she got almost to his chair,
she stopped and waited.

He was very still. Too still!

She stared at him. His head was listing. His mouth
was slack. She couldn't see any sign that his chest was
moving up and down.

Oh, God! She'd given him too many pills. He wasn't
breathing. The combination of drugs and liquor had
been lethal.

Chapter Nine

She let out a cry and raced to him. His empty coffee cup lay beside the chair. *He had drunk every last drop!* She put her ear against his chest. With a grateful sob she knew that he was still breathing, but each intake was very shallow.

"Wake up! Wake up!" She slapped his face and his dark eyelashes flickered slightly on his closed eyes.

She had to get help. Nothing else was important. All thoughts of getting away were lost in the upheaval of saving his life. She turned and grabbed the phone, but before she could dial, there was a rush of air behind her.

"Game's over," he growled as he raised up behind her and pinned her arms at her sides.

"What?" For an instant utter relief swamped everything else. *He was all right.* She hadn't killed him.

He spun her around. "Surprise, surprise."

"You're not...not..." she gasped.

"Knocked out? Dead? Sorry to disappoint you."

Fury as she'd never known before surged through her. She spat a string of swearwords she didn't even know were in her vocabulary.

"Lady, lady, what language." He jerked her to him and his strong hands splayed across her back and waist, "Next time you try putting something in my drink make sure there isn't a mirror behind the bar. I saw your sly little performance and poured my coffee back in the pot. What did you put in it?"

"Sleeping pills." Her anger dissipated, replaced by horror as she admitted what she'd done. She couldn't believe that she had taken such chances with another person's life. If anyone deserved to be scared out of her skin, she did. Looking up into his glowering handsome face, she said honestly, "I'm glad you didn't drink it."

"Really?" He raised an eyebrow doubtfully.

"Yes, really." She was aware of the wonderful rhythm of his breathing and the reassurance of his warm breath upon her face. His hands trailed up her arms until his fingers rested lightly around the open collar of her blouse.

"I should wring your neck for trying such a stunt," he said. There was the softly caressing and strangely sensual touch of his fingertips upon her skin. His dark eyes searched her face as his hands slipped to her shoulders, pulling her closer. "You really want me out of the way, don't you?"

"Not like that."

"I don't understand. You set me up so you could get away, but when you thought I was asleep, you stayed and tried to wake me."

"I thought I'd killed you. I forgot about everything else."

His eyes narrowed. "That's hard to believe."

"It's true. I couldn't leave you like that." She reached up and touched his cheek. It felt wonderfully warm and alive. Her heart was suddenly racing, and a joy she didn't understand sluiced through her. He moved his head slightly so that his lips placed a kiss on her fingertips as she traced the curve of his chin. The contact was gentle, fleeting, but his eyes held a compelling intensity that locked her in its grip. His hands slid down to the curve of her hips and he pressed her against his heat. She lifted her face, closed her eyes, but his mouth never found hers.

His hands dropped abruptly away and she heard him swear. Her eyes flew open. Damas was staring at the door she had insisted they leave open.

Malchek stood there, knocking with a heavy fist. His thick walrus frame filled the doorway and an ugly smirk creased his face. Alexa felt his gaze go all over her like something slimy. She knew that the heat of physical arousal was in her face. She didn't dare look at Damas, whose rigidity communicated his discomfort.

"Sorry to intrude," Malchek sneered.

"What in the hell do you want?" snapped Damas.

"I was just wondering if you'd be needing the limo tomorrow, Mrs. Santini."

Malchek's gaze slid over the dinner cart and dirty dishes, and the man's malevolence came at her stronger than ever.

Somehow she found her voice. "No, I don't want the car. Please take the day off. I won't be needing you."

His pudgy lips curved in a malicious smile. "Thank you, ma'am. You'll let me know if you change your mind, won't you? I wouldn't want—"

"She said she wouldn't need you," Damas cut in, and strode toward the door. He towered over Malchek by a head and the chauffeur stepped back.

"I didn't mean to interrupt anything," Malchek said with a snigger.

"You didn't," Damas answered curtly. "Otherwise the door would have been shut." Damas's stony expression dared any argument.

Malchek shrugged his thick shoulders, but there was no concession in his hard little eyes as he gave Alexa one last stabbing stare, and she read the message clear enough: *You two don't fool me none.*

Much to Alexa's dismay, Damas followed him out of the suite and closed the door behind them. She sank down on the sofa and put her head in her hands. She felt like someone who had been tossed out of a plane at thirty thousand feet.

DAMAS SILENTLY CURSED Malchek as he punched the elevator button and then stood waiting with his thick shoulders like those of a hunched baboon. A formidable enemy. He had put Malchek on the defensive and that could mean big, big trouble. No doubt Malchek's snooping had helped send Guy to his final swim in the river. Blast it all. He had to defuse the situation somehow. And quick. Lies had never sat well with him, but he had no choice. A lot could be at stake— including his life.

He gave Malchek a man-to-man wink. "That gal is some sexy barracuda. I thought I could handle any broad, but she sure duped me."

"Looked like you were doing all right," Malchek said without changing his pugnacious expression.

"Nah. I fell for an invitation to a quiet dinner and then pow! Any man with blood in his veins would forget for a moment that she's the boss's wife. But I knew better than to follow up on her overtures. When you knocked she was trying to get me to kiss her. Hell, looking after her is like holding on to a stick of dynamite. I can see now why Guy Lentz wanted out of the job."

"Is that what you think? I guess you haven't seen tonight's paper." Malchek gave a satisfied grunt.

Damas knew what was coming. Mia's bodyguard had stepped over the line. Damas tried to keep his expression bland as he shook his head. "No. What's happening?"

"Guy had an accident this afternoon. Been drinking, they say. Ran his car straight off the road into the East River." A satisfied glint showed in Malchek's eyes. "I kept telling him he ought to be more careful. You know what I mean?"

Damas knew exactly what he meant, but he parried the razor-edged question. "Tell me about this gal, Malchek. Is Mia Santini up to her usual tricks? Has more than one of her bodyguards met with an unfortunate accident?"

His thick lips curved. "Just one—so far." He stepped into the elevator. "But, hell, that could change.Know what I mean?" The doors slammed shut on his crude laugh.

Damas listened to the whine of the descending elevator. Malchek's parting thrust was a warning, one Damas couldn't afford to ignore. If he crossed Leo and lost good standing with the Santini organization, he'd be another dead duck in the water. He was furious with himself. Why had he gone into Mia's suite? His lack of judgment had given her the opportunity to drug his coffee. What was worse, she had totally aroused him. He had wanted to caress her full ripe breasts and feel her quivering body against his. The lips she'd offered him had driven everything else out of his mind. Malchek's inopportune arrival had stopped him from kissing her, but the chauffeur had seen them in a lovers' embrace that could jeopardize everything.

Damas plowed his hand through his hair. He was tempted to storm back into the suite and shake her till his anger was spent—but he knew he didn't dare. He failed to understand what was going on in that devious mind of hers. She could have left him without a backward glance when she'd thought he was out from the drugged coffee. Instead she had slapped his face, cried his name and had been ready to phone for help, when he'd stopped her. Her eyes had filled with tears of relief. Why? When he knew she would go to any lengths to get away?

She's a manipulator, an inner voiced warned. One man had died today because of her seductive powers. She was in for a bad time when her husband arrived, but damned if he'd play any more games with her. Long ago he'd learned to value his own skin. He stuck to business and steered clear of entanglements. He cursed himself for allowing his emotions to get involved. He knew better. Nobody crossed Leo Santini and got away with it.

He heard the muffled sound of a telephone ringing in her suite. Maybe Leo was calling to see how his pretty little wife was getting along.

ALEXA RAISED her head. Her heart began racing and her mouth was instantly parched. Should she let the phone ring? What if it was Leo checking on Mia? What would he think if she wasn't in her room at this late hour? Could she fake her sister's end of the conversation? She doubted that the phone was bugged, since Santini hadn't ever been at the hotel. With cold sweat coating her hand, she picked up the receiver and managed a sleepy "Hello."

"You're still there! You said you'd get the baby and come back right away," wailed her sister. "I've been out of my mind. Going crazy waiting and waiting." Her voice took on a peevish edge. "Don't you know it's almost midnight?"

"Yes, I—"

"You sound sleepy. What's going on? Aren't you coming? You should have been here by now. Why didn't you call me? Why didn't—"

"Mia! If you'll shut up for a minute, I'll tell you. I'm still here because I haven't been able to get away from your husband's watchdog. Every time I think I can get Dorrie and get out of this place, he's always two jumps ahead of me."

"He can't watch you every minute!"

"That's what I thought. I didn't see him anywhere, so I went to get the baby and he was standing by her crib. He's figured out that I'm not leaving without

Dorrie." Alexa related the drugged-coffee debacle. "I really thought I'd put his life in danger with alcohol and those sleeping pills of yours."

"I wish you had."

"Mia!" The horror of that frightening moment when she'd thought he wasn't breathing still stabbed her. "You can't mean that."

After a reluctant silence, Mia said, "I guess not. I just wish your plan had worked and you were on your way to me with the baby. I don't know how much more of this I can stand."

"Do you want to call off the impersonation? Come back and take your chances with Leo?"

"I can't," she wailed.

"Maybe things would go better than you think," Alexa offered, with little conviction.

"Guy's dead." Mia gave a choked sob. "I loved him and now he's dead. The paper called it an accident. Ran his car into the river. But it was Leo's doing. They made it look like he was drunk. Don't you see? He'll destroy anyone or anything I care about. He's never allowed anyone to love me...not even an innocent puppy or stray cat. Now he'll carry out his threats about keeping Dorrie from me. He could give orders to take her away any minute. Tomorrow may be too late. You have to do something, Alexa. You have to hurry...."

"I've tried...God knows how I've tried. Nothing works."

"Can't you sweet-talk this new bodyguard to look the other way? Men are men, you know. Take him to bed and—!"

"Mia! I couldn't." Heat came up into Alexa's cheeks with the denial. She remembered how she had leaned into Damas's embrace, enveloped in a bursting spiral of wild desire. She'd never reacted to a man on such a purely physical level before and she couldn't account for her bewildering behavior, but it had not been motivated by any intent on her part to best him.

"Did Leo ever mention Damas Silva?" she asked impulsively.

"Silva...Silva," repeated Mia. "I remember Leo mentioning his name a few times, but I—" Her voice cracked. "Oh, my God. I remember now. Alexa, you have to be careful. He's dangerous. He killed someone."

Alexa's stomach took a sickening plunge. Her breath was short. "Who...who did he kill?"

"A federal agent...something went wrong at a pickup. One of Leo's men was shot to death at the same time."

"Why wasn't Silva arrested?"

"Leo was bragging about how smart Damas Silva was...smarter than the detectives handling the case. They never charged him with anything. Alexa, what are you going to do? If you cross this guy the wrong way, he might really hurt you. I'm afraid...really afraid. Maybe you should walk out of the place right now."

"How can I? Unless you're ready to give up Dorrie?"

"But what are you going to do?"

"Mia, I honestly don't know. I forged your name on a credit slip for some clothes. I'm going to need money—"

"There's a hundred-dollar bill under one of Dorrie's photos in my purse. Mad money."

"Thank heavens. That will help, but no taxi driver is going to make that kind of change. I'll have to get it broken.

"It's hopeless, isn't it?" A frightening calmness replaced the rising hysteria that had been there a moment before in Mia's voice. "Leo always wins."

"He hasn't won yet," Alexa said quickly. "Don't give up. I'll try again tomorrow. How much time do I have before Leo arrives?"

"I don't know. He never tells me anything. He said a few days. That's all I know."

"Will he telephone?"

"He never does. Just shows up. Expects me to be there, all smiles and dutiful. I never know what mood he'll be in." Her voice quivered. "This time it will be worse than ever. He'll get his revenge...."

"We still have time," Alexa reassured her, silently praying she was right. She had to change tactics. There wasn't any chance she could sneak by Damas. He was alerted to her determination to take the baby and leave. She'd have to trick him. But at the moment she was too emotionally exhausted to put two thoughts together. "I can't do anything more tonight, but I'll do my best to bring the baby to you tomorrow. Is Mrs. Trimble looking after you?"

"Yes. She's a dear. Been in and out all day. Soaked my foot. Wrapped my ankle. I can't put my weight on it yet. I just lie here and worry. Are you sure Dorrie's all right?"

"She's fine. Now, get some sleep. We'll have to figure out what to do when I get back." The big bouquet of roses scattered on the floor caught her eye. "Do you know a Frank Zurick?"

"I know *of* him. A big shot in a Chicago syndicate. Leo's been fighting his attempt to expand into the New York area. Hates his guts. Why?"

"I'm afraid I may have unwittingly done something that will have unfortunate repercussions. He bought me a drink and I agreed to have dinner with him—"

"With Frank Zurick?" Mia moaned. "Why on earth would you do such a thing? Leo would kill me for even talking to him. If he hears that I was drinking with his arch enemy, he'll be furious."

"I'm sorry. A bad mistake. I'm trying to cope in an impossible situation, when I haven't the foggiest idea what to say or do."

"Well, I don't understand why you were spending time drinking and eating!" Mia lashed out.

"I was doing my best pretending to be you, party girl!" Alexa responded curtly. "It wasn't my idea to play the social butterfly. I only did what was expected. Clara let me know you always dressed up in the evening and joined some merrymaking group. I figured I'd pretend to drink enough to make Silva think I'd retired with a load for the night."

"And you hooked up with Zurick, of all people?"

"I had no idea who he was. I met him in the lounge. He was friendly, charming. I was trying to fill up the evening, so I accepted his invitation to dinner. We were on our way to the dining room, when Damas saw me with Zurick. He faked a telephone call from Leo to get me away."

"I shudder to think what my husband would do if he learned that Zurick came on to me," wailed Mia. "He'd have to avenge his pride. For heaven's sake stay clear of that man."

"Don't worry. I'll stay in my suite until I work out a plan to get away. Try to get some sleep. As I said, there's nothing I can do until morning. With luck I'll see you before tomorrow night. Promise me you won't do anything foolish, Mia. There has to be a way out of this mess, and I intend to find it."

She hung up the phone without the slightest clue as to how she was going to make good on such a declaration.

Chapter Ten

Alexa was certain she was too strung out to sleep, but sunshine outlined the edges of the bedroom draperies when she awoke the next morning with a start. She sat up. Her body was suffused with a tingling heat and her breasts felt full and tender. A spiral of desire lingered. She was appalled when she realized that she had been dreaming about Damas lying naked beside her, enfolding her in his muscular arms. The fantasy of his kisses cruising over her skin lingered with disturbing vividness.

With a muttered "Damn" she threw back the covers and headed for the bathroom. She let the hard spray of water sting her face. What on earth was the matter with her? She couldn't believe the intensity of longing. Her erotic dreams dismayed her. With a force of will, she quickly buried them, determined that she wouldn't allow herself to give them even the slightest recognition. She pulled her thoughts in a different direction. Nothing had seemed real since Mia's frantic knock on her door. No, she mentally corrected herself; the threatening Damas Silva was very real. The truth had dispelled any illusions about him. Her bodyguard was a Santini man...and a killer.

She shivered and reached for a towel.

She surveyed Mia's wardrobe and chose a designer jumpsuit in soft pink and a pair of white sandals. Then she brushed her hair into a shiny golden flip that curved gently on her shoulders. As she applied her makeup, she decided only a woman with nothing to do would have the time to use all the cosmetics Mia had packed. She examined her appearance carefully in the mirror, and decided she would pass for her sister once again.

She called room service and ate breakfast while she stared out the window at the lake. There had to be a way to give Damas the slip. She didn't know how, but whenever the opportunity arose, she had to be ready to seize it and get away from the resort with the baby as quickly as possible. Maybe an escape would present itself when she became more familiar with the hotel and its grounds.

She set down her coffee cup, took a deep breath and rose to her feet. First of all, she needed to get Dorrie. She had to have the baby in her possession if she was to be ready to take advantage of any unexpected situations that came her way.

When she opened the door of her suite, Damas was sitting in a chair, finishing off a last bite of toast. In spite of her determination to put her erotic fantasies from her mind, she felt heat seeping into her face. Her eyes undressed him as the memory of his naked body came thrashing back, destroying her equilibrium.

He set his breakfast tray aside when he saw her and stood up. "Good morning," he said pleasantly.

He was freshly shaven and a whiff of men's cologne touched her nostrils. Shiny black wavy hair glistened from a recent shampoo. He wore white pants and a blue sport shirt, open at the collar to show an expanse of tan skin a shade lighter than his bare arms. He looked refreshed and as ready as any gladiator for the day's challenges. Apparently he had not spent the night on guard patrol, a truth that irritated her. Had she passed up an opportunity to slip away then?

"Did you have a good night's sleep?" he asked.

"Yes, thank you." He wasn't going to throw her off balance with his conviviality. She knew him for what he was.

"And pleasant dreams?" A corner of his mouth lifted, as if he had been privy to her fantasy.

"Just a nightmare or two." Her eyes met his and then jerked away.

Damas was intrigued. *I'll be damned,* he thought. The hot little scene between them last night had gotten to her. The lady was acting embarrassed. What an act. She was good, damn good, but Mia Santini's reputation was not one of unsullied womanhood. Hell, she could turn a man inside out and laugh while she was doing it. Take Guy Lentz, for instance. A flare of anger engulfed him and he said curtly, "I don't know if I should be the one to tell you about your former bodyguard—"

"I know . . . what happened."

He raised an eyebrow.

Alexa was aware that Mia would have expressed a lover's anguish, but the best she could do was substitute anger. "It wasn't an accident. You know it and so do I! Guy was killed . . . murdered. But you know all

about that, don't you? Do all of Leo's men move up
the ranks when they kill someone?''

She had the satisfaction of seeing a flash like a blade
shoot through his dark eyes. She'd drawn blood with
the remark, yet she realized that the thrust had been
foolish. She was no match for the kind of ruthless men
Leo employed. She started past him, but he grabbed
her arm and tightened his fingers.

"I think you're the one who can take credit for
Guy's misfortune."

Alexa wanted more than anything to step out of her
sister's shoes at that moment. The sins of her twin
weighed heavily upon her. She wanted to break free of
the tangled mesh that wasn't of her making, but all she
could do was pull away from him without answering.
What could she say? He was horribly right. If Mia
hadn't betrayed her husband, Guy would probably
still be alive. Damas had every right to look at her with
contempt.

It doesn't matter what he thinks of you, she told
herself as she walked across the sitting room. The
memory of his legs entwined with hers and the soft
touch of his kisses was still strong enough to shoot a
bewildering flush through her. She found her cheeks
were burning. *Keep your mind on getting away from
him. After today, you'll probably never see him again.*
For the first time she focused on the repercussions he'd
face when Leo arrived at Foxfire and found his wife
gone. *Don't think about that.* Being Santini's henchman was his choice of occupation and without a doubt
he'd learned how to handle Leo before this.

Clara had set the playpen up in the sitting room and
Dorrie was lying in it, contentedly chewing on a rubber

teething ring as she kicked her feet and slobbered. The nanny was reclining on a sofa, reading a magazine, and she heaved herself into a sitting position as Alexa came in. The woman's expression was about as warm as a dripping icicle.

Alexa ignored her brittle glare and smiled at her. "I'm going to take Dorrie out in the stroller this morning. That will give you a few free hours to yourself."

Whatever Clara was about to say got caught in her thick throat. Her stony stare softened. Getting rid of the baby for a morning obviously appealed to her.

She gave her double chin a toss. "I was going to take her out myself, but if you want to..." Her voice trailed off.

"I'll need a diaper bag and a bottle or two. I don't know how long we'll be gone. Where's the stroller?"

Clara nodded toward the bedroom and waddled into the room ahead of Alexa. While she packed the bag, Alexa pushed the stroller into the sitting room and parked it by the playpen. Leaning over the railing, she awkwardly took the baby out. Dorrie shoved the teething ring into Alexa's face with one hand, and with the other her chubby little fingers caught a hank of Alexa's hair.

"Ouch!" Alexa tried to shift the wiggling baby and hold on to her as she tried to extricate her hair from her niece's fists. "Let go...ouch...let go."

Her voice must have carried through the open hall door, because Damas chuckled as he came into the room and saw the situation. He took Dorrie and gently tried to pry the little fist open. He was successful, but not before the baby had given Alexa's hair some good yanks.

"Don't scalp your mother," he said.

Mother! What a laugh. She was as adept a mother as a wrestler dancing a minuet. She knew Damas was enjoying himself as she rubbed her head.

Clara came in with the diaper bag and fastened it on the back of the stroller. Thank heavens, thought Alexa. She never would have known where to put the bulky thing.

Damas continued to hold the baby, murmuring something, and Dorrie gave him an openmouthed, slobbery smile. Talk about feeling like a third wheel, thought Alexa. She not only felt inadequate, but uneasy. Was Damas deliberately mocking her? Had he picked up on her total lack of maternal competence?

Mia would have taken charge of her baby, but Alexa hesitated. The fancy stroller presented a challenge in itself. It was a mine field for someone who had never put a baby in one. A retreat was in order.

"I forgot something. When you get through playing, put Dorrie in the stroller and bring her out to the elevator." Alexa turned on her heel and made a quick exit. She came out of the suite a few minutes later, having taken the opportunity to double-check Mia's purse for the one hundred dollars. Now she needed to get it changed into smaller denominations. She could use Mia's credit card for expenses like airfare, but she couldn't tip taxi drivers and redcaps with only a large bill. Maybe she could distract Damas with the baby long enough to buy something in one of the shops.

She felt strangely calm and collected when she joined him at the elevator. Clara had put a pink sunbonnet on Dorrie and someone—probably Damas—had tied her rubber teething ring to the stroller tray.

Damas deftly maneuvered the stroller into the elevator, and as Alexa stood beside him and the baby on the way down, a bewildering sensation flowed over her. *They looked like a family.* Long, lonely years were swept away as a circle of warmth seemed to draw the three of them together in the absurd fantasy. When the elevator door slid open on the ground floor, reality came back with a start.

As soon as they were out of the elevator, Alexa took control of the stroller. "Thank you," she said briskly. "I can manage."

The dismissal in her tone was unmistakable. "I take it that you want me walking ten steps behind or not at all."

"Not at all would be best," she said bluntly.

"Dream on, Mrs. Santini. I won't crowd you, but I'll be around. Close enough to see everything . . . and protect you." His lips curved in a mocking smile that was purely chauvinistic. "Frankly, you give the impression that you need a great deal of . . . protection."

"From you . . . or someone else?" She saw a rise of color under the tan of his neck, and felt a smug sense of satisfaction. They both knew that he had been ready to kiss her when Malchek had interrupted. The knowledge gave her a foolish sense of feminine superiority, even though in her heart she knew she'd been the one leaning into his embrace. The memory made her angry and she tightened her grip on the stroller.

Alexa pushed Dorrie quickly across the lobby and into a gift shop, intent upon getting the hundred-dollar bill changed into smaller denominations.

She discovered almost immediately that the aisles were too narrow for the stroller. After negotiating a frustrating corner, she parked the baby and hurriedly went over to a counter displaying overpriced stuffed animals. Alexa searched to find the least expensive one. She grabbed up a small pink elephant marked fifteen dollars and looked around for a clerk.

She heard an "Eek!" from the saleslady before she turned around and saw her making a dash to the spot where Alexa had parked the stroller.

"No...no," the older woman shrieked.

Alexa saw with horror that Dorrie had managed to reach out and grab an arrangement of silk flowers on a nearby shelf that was on her level. She was happily pulling the bouquet apart, absorbed in tearing off green leaves and stuffing crumbled red blossoms into her mouth.

The saleslady wrestled away the desecrated bouquet. Alexa got the red petals out of Dorrie's mouth, but not before her mouth had been dyed a vivid crimson. The baby gazed up at Alexa, chortling happily and looking like a painted doll with her red lips.

"I'm so sorry," Alexa said, picking up the debris from the floor.

The saleswoman didn't bat an eye as she held out the sales tag for the silk flower arrangement. "Thirty-nine ninety-eight. Do you want it wrapped?"

Alexa managed a feeble smile as she shook her head. If she'd been thinking clearly, she would have put the stuffed toy back and just paid for the ruined flowers. With the pink elephant, her purchases came to fifty-five dollars. That meant she was left with less than half of the hundred-dollar bill. Given that she had no idea how much money she might need, forty-five dollars was a miserable amount of cash.

She handed Dorrie the elephant and pushed the stroller out of the store as quickly as she could. In the lobby, she looked around for Damas, but she didn't see him. She hoped he hadn't witnessed the embarrassing fiasco in the store. Just thinking about his amusement, she felt her chin lift in a pugnacious tilt. Still, the first thing on her list had been accomplished, however unsatisfactorily. Next she needed to familiarize herself with the hotel layout. She headed toward the front entrance.

A doorman tipped his gold-braided hat as she came out the glass doors. "Have a nice day."

The phrase had never seemed so banal. A landscaped walk led around the building and Alexa made note of a taxi station just beyond the opening of an underground parking area. At one end of the hotel, a group of people were preparing to climb into some old-fashioned carriages and tallyho wagons. Alexa remembered a flyer in the suite about the hotel offering sight-seeing tours, but at the time she'd paid little attention. Now she realized that such an excursion might provide a means of getting away.

She turned around and searched the crowd and sidewalk for Damas. No sign of him. Maybe he had been confident that she wasn't going anywhere when she passed up the taxi station and hotel shuttle bus.

Quickly she scooped Dorrie out of the stroller. Where was the pink elephant? The baby had been flinging it around by the trunk and she must have dropped it somewhere along the way.

She shifted Dorrie to one arm and slid the heavy diaper bag over the other. Weighted down, she gave her suite number to a hotel attendant. He parked the stroller for her in a small enclosure and then helped her climb into a tallyho, a tall wagon with wooden benches that seated about a dozen people. She took the first empty bench. The wagon was covered with a tarp and its open sides gave a clear view of the surroundings.

She looked back toward the front of the hotel. Still no sign of Damas. Maybe he hadn't seen her join the excursion crowd. Sitting in the middle of the wagon, she wasn't clearly visible. With luck she would remain obscured by other people. Comforted, she settled Dorrie on her lap and placed the diaper bag on the floor. The wagon was almost full and Alexa saw with relief that the driver of the tallyho was preparing to get underway.

"Such a darling baby," cooed a chubby, white-haired woman in the bench seat behind her. She leaned forward and tickled Dorrie under her chin. "Reminds me of our second granddaughter. The same blue eyes."

Alexa gave her a vague smile.

"What's her name?"

Alexa was about to answer, when she was stopped by a tanned hand waving a stuffed pink elephant in her face.

"I think you dropped this."

Damas slid onto the bench across the narrow aisle. Dorrie gave him a toothless smile as she stuffed the pink trunk in her mouth, but Alexa turned her face away and stared unseeing out the open wagon.

Tears of utter frustration welled in the corners of her eyes. She should have known that he'd never let her leave the hotel grounds without him tagging along. What should she do now? Before she could give in to the impulse to flee the wagon, the driver shouted "Giddyap," and the heavy Clydesdale horses set the huge wooden wheels in motion.

The decision had been taken from her. All right, she told herself. No need to panic. Undoubtedly some stops would be made along the way on this sight-seeing tour. She might be able to give him the slip then, and by the time he got back to the hotel, she could be gone. Buoyed by this possibility, she felt the taut knot in her stomach ease.

Dorrie liked the bouncing of the wagon and she settled back against Alexa's chest, looking up at her from time to time with a gurgling smile that made every discomfort in the world well worth it. Alexa took a deep breath and managed to relax a little, even though she was more aware of Damas than she wanted to be. She didn't look at him directly, yet his long legs, which eased out into the small aisle, teased her with their nearness. The remembered warmth of his limbs pressed against hers set her mouth in a hard line. She was aware of his gaze upon her and it was all she could do to ignore him. She had been a fool last night. He wouldn't find her that vulnerable today. She would do what she had to do.

The huge wagon continued to bounce from side to side. Dorrie didn't mind a bit, but Alexa thought the board benches were hard and uncomfortable. She hoped it wasn't very far to the first stop.

"Are we having fun yet?" Damas inquired sarcastically.

"No one asked you to come," she answered sweetly.

A pretty girl dressed in an old-fashioned dimity dress and sunbonnet stood up and began reciting a speech about the new Foxfire Resort, directing their gaze to an old tower built on a high ridge above the lake. The girl smiled at Damas.

"The view from the lookout is spectacular...the Catskill Mountains to the west and the Berkshires northeast. A perfect place for lunch," she said with an inviting smile.

Lunch! With a sickening jerk, Alexa realized that the carriages and wagons were headed up the mountainside to the lookout building. She was trapped. The isolated spot would offer nothing in the way of an escape. Why on earth had she ever left the hotel?

Chapter Eleven

"This ought to be interesting," said Damas dryly as the driver reined the horses to a stop in front of the old rock lookout building, which had been modernized to provide refreshments, rest rooms and a safe staircase to climb to the top of the tower.

"I'm glad you approve," she said sarcastically. "Although it really doesn't matter, since you came along uninvited." She landed with force on the last word.

"Just doing my job. As a bodyguard I guard bodies—in this case yours—whether you like it or not."

She just glared at him and tried to draw away when he offered a hand down from the high step. She couldn't move with her usual gracefulness because she had the baby in her arms and the diaper bag dangling off one shoulder and she almost stumbled. As he steadied her, he could feel the soft warmth of her body through the thin fabric of her jumpsuit and he cursed an involuntary sexual response. *Shut it off, Silva.*

"Give me the baby," he growled.

"No!" She pulled away from him. "I . . . I have to change her," she said, grasping at this motherly excuse to get away from him. She needed some space. She couldn't think when every sense was attuned to his nearness.

Picnic tables were scattered in an open area in front of the tower, overlooking the lake and hotel far below. As the passengers unloaded from the various wagons and carriages, hotel personnel quickly brought out box lunches and a variety of beverages.

Without a backward glance Alexa headed into the stone building and found the rest room. It had a changing table, and even though Alexa was less than efficient, the disposable diapers were easy to handle. Dorrie bent her fat little legs and played with her feet. Somewhere along the way, she'd lost one of her booties. Impulsively, Alexa nibbled at the pink little toes and Dorrie laughed loudly, waving her arms excitedly.

"She is a darling," cooed the same grandmotherly looking woman who had sat behind them. "How old is she?"

"She's five months."

"What a bright little thing. She's got your beautiful blue eyes. Going to be as pretty as her mother." The woman sighed. "I wish mine were all little again. They grow up too fast. Enjoy her while you can. You don't want to miss a single moment."

"I know," said Alexa. The woman's words had a special meaning for Alexa and a sense of urgency settled on her again.

When she came outside, she didn't see Damas at first. Then he stood up and waved to her from one of the tables placed along the rim of the rocky bluff. She hesitated. Sitting that close to the drop-off was unnerving enough and she wasn't certain that she wanted to share a table with the man she was trying to elude.

Dorrie made the decision for her. With a wail, she let Alexa know that it was time for her lunch, as well. The baby thrashed wildly in Alexa's arms, screaming louder and louder. Dorrie was angelic most of the time, but she threw a fit when she was hungry. Alexa felt as if everybody in the milling crowd was looking at her. She quickened her steps and dropped the diaper bag off her shoulder onto the table beside Damas.

"Sounds like she's ready for a bottle," said Damas, digging into the bag. When he located one in an isolated pouch, he took it out. "Here, let me have her."

Alexa gave up the screaming infant without a murmur and sank down on the bench beside him.

"I come from a large family, remember?" A hard glint crossed his eyes. "And we didn't have nursemaids." He cradled Dorrie in one arm and popped the bottle in her mouth. In a split second the baby's cries changed to slurps of pleasure.

His handling Dorrie the way he did made her feel totally inadequate—not a feeling that she'd had very many times in her life. If anything, she'd always been too competent, too much in control of every situation. The fact that he consistently showed her up when it came to caring for Dorrie was utterly demoralizing. She knew she was being sexist in her attitude, but men weren't supposed to be the nurturing ones. Especially not men who carried guns, killed people and made a living working for a mob boss. This dangerous man kept her completely off stride, and if she failed to checkmate him in this game they were playing, her sister might have to give up the baby forever.

A cool breeze touched her face and she realized that her cheeks were flushed. Her hair was an untidy mess and she longed to pull it back out of the way in a schoolmarm twist. When her gaze wandered over the high precipice down to the lake, she felt herself blanch, and unconsciously she gripped the edge of the table.

"You don't like heights, I take it," Damas commented.

"No," she admitted. "Not since I was traveling with my parents in Switzerland when I was ten years old and a cable car failed and we were left dangling for hours over a chasm." The second the last word was out, she swallowed a hard knot in her throat. *That was Alexa Widmire's memory—not Mia Santini's.*

Damas raised a dark eyebrow, wondering why she had gone all rigid. He had the feeling the reason was more than just an unpleasant memory, but he couldn't put his finger on it. "I had a similar experience once," he said smoothly. "Only mine was a dangling fire escape that broke loose from an old building in the Lower East Side. I couldn't go up or down for hours until the firemen got there—but I didn't mind. I liked surveying the world from a lofty position."

Is that why he'd gotten himself mixed up with Santini? she wondered. So he could look down at the world? Money. Power. A chance to be more than a poor kid? What a waste, she thought, and for a moment she allowed herself a foolish "what if." What if things were different? What if they had met under different circumstances?

Stop it! Where was her common sense? Indulging in such fantasizing was like holding a bomb that was ready to explode. She had to remain detached where he was concerned. Not an easy thing to do when he carefully lifted the sleeping baby to his shoulder and patted her back. Dorrie obliged with a loud burp. Alexa knew her eyes were softer than they should be as she and Damas exchanged smiles.

They spread the baby blanket out on the table and very gently Damas placed Dorrie on her tummy. Her little arms lay relaxed above her head like a ballerina's and long lashes feathered her pink cheeks. Alexa bent down and kissed the spot where a fringe of fair hair edged her niece's tiny forehead. A swell of love twisted Alexa's heartstrings and she bit her lower lip to hold back a flood of emotion.

"You're a strange one," Damas said quietly, watching her. His gaze slid from her soft, moist eyes and down the sweet lines of her cheeks and quivering chin. In spite of himself he kept remembering the way she had pressed against him and lifted her face for a kiss. He'd never had a woman ignite a sexual hunger the way she did. All night he'd wrestled with the heat of wanting her. *Don't be a fool,* he lectured himself. *She's a package of feminine dynamite that'll blow up in your face.*

"How about some lunch?" he asked gruffly, and handed her one of the boxes left at their table. "Aren't you hungry?" he demanded when she just sat there, looking at some distant point across the valley.

She shook her head and rose to her feet. "I'll be back in a minute."

He watched her glide purposefully toward the rock tower. "What's she up to now?" he asked under his breath. He was pretty sure that she wouldn't leave without the baby—but not positive. After last night's attempt to drug him, he couldn't dismiss anything she did as innocent. He pushed his uneaten lunch aside. A rigid self-control had kept him all in one piece so far. No seductive female was worth the gamble that he'd end up with his feet in a bucket of cement and dumped in the river.

Where in the hell was she? He was about to get to his feet, when he felt a prickling on the back of his neck. He instinctively dropped his right hand to his side, freeing it to reach for the gun in his side holster. In his business, you went with your instincts...and watched your back if you wanted to celebrate your next birthday. Slowly he turned around and let his eyes rake the area behind him. No one at the nearby picnic table was looking in his direction.

As his gaze roved upward, he caught a movement in one of the high apertures of the tower. The distance was too great to make out a face, but he was positive he had been under surveillance from that high opening. Adrenaline rushed through him. The tower provided a sniper with a perfect shot. If he'd seen a glint of a gun, he would have dived to the ground.

He took a couple of steps away from the table and then stopped. Damn! The baby. He couldn't leave Dorrie alone. Where was Mia? Not in the tower, if she truly hated heights. Had someone whisked her out from under his nose? Zurick? The Chicago gangster would be capable of a forceful pursuit, even adding abduction to settle the score with Leo.

Damas scooped up the sleeping baby and plopped her in the arms of a grandmotherly looking woman chattering and laughing at the next table.

"Good heavens," she gasped.

"Watch her for me," Damas ordered, as he took off for the tower at a dead run.

The stairway to the tower was inside the building and sightseers were coming and going from every direction.

He took the stone steps two at a time, urging other climbers out of the way as he bounded upward. At the top, a square observation deck provided a view in all four directions. He saw nothing except the man who leaned up against a parapet, smoking a cigarette.

"Nice view," Malchek said with a smirk.

The top of Damas's head exploded with anger. "What in the hell are you doing here?"

"Same thing you are."

"I don't get it," Damas retorted, but he did. *Watchdog watching the watchdog.*

Damas's earlier suspicion came back full blown. Had Leo set him up with this bodyguard assignment...ordered Malchek to watch him? To prove what? That Mia Santini would play around with any man in her proximity? He knew that an account of this little sight-seeing jaunt would find its way into Malchek's report. No doubt he would twist it into some kind of a lovers' rendezvous. Malchek's malicious little eyes confirmed it.

"Got a thing for the lady, have ya?" the ugly man baited.

"Stuff it! It's only a job," he answered bluntly, trying to ignore a deep mocking truth. *It had become much more than that.* He knew that it wouldn't take much for an ape like Malchek to come up with the right score. "Just a job."

"Some job," mocked Malchek.

"Listen good, Malchek. I'll be damned if I'll play games with you. I saw you spying on us and thought it might be Zurick or one of his men. Because of you, I've left the baby and Mrs. Santini unattended." Damas stuck his angry face so close to Malchek's that he cowered against the stone wall. "Get this straight! Any trouble you cause for me or Mrs. Santini will come straight home to roost. And any filthy lies you spread to the boss I'll personally cram down that thick gullet of yours. Got it?"

Malchek set his pudgy mouth in a hard line. "I tell what I see. And what I'm seeing ain't pretty."

"Then get yourself a pair of glasses before you end up with two black eyes and a broken nose." With that threat, Damas turned away and bounded down the stone steps.

He couldn't find her. No sign of her in the small coffee shop or gift store. He asked a woman coming out of the ladies' room if his blond girlfriend was still in there. She shook her head.

Again he wondered, had someone spirited her away? Or had she run away on her own? He'd always been sure she wouldn't leave without the baby. He froze. Maybe she'd come back while he was with Malchek, picked up Dorrie and taken off. Some of the carriages had already departed.

He rushed out the door... and nearly knocked her down as she came around the corner of the building. Her hair was combed and she had freshened her lipstick. He felt like a perfect fool under her appraising eyes. His mad search had left him tense and slightly breathless. He wanted to grab her by the shoulders and shake her. Or better still, kiss her until her luscious mouth was bruised and pliable.

"You thought I'd given you the slip, didn't you?" She smiled as if she had made points over an opponent. "I just took a little stroll to clear my head. You should know I wouldn't leave without the baby." A flash of anxiety crossed her face. "Where's Dorrie?"

"I left her with a . . . a nice lady."

Alexa looked horrified. "You left Dorrie with a perfect stranger?"

"Had no choice. I had to take care of something." He took Alexa's arm. "Come on, let's go get her."

He set a quick pace with his long legs. As Alexa kept up with him, she sensed an explosive tension within him. She wanted to ask Damas what was so urgent that he'd left the baby with a stranger, but the glower on his face stopped her. A different kind of fear sped through her. Not for herself, but for him. One man had lost his life because of Mia Santini. Alexa's stomach took a sickening plunge. Was she putting Damas in the same kind of danger?

When the pink-cheeked woman caught sight of Alexa, she smiled broadly. Dorrie was sleeping happily in her arms. "I thought this was your baby. She's such a dear. Been sleeping like an angel the whole time." Her smile wavered as she looked from Alexa's worried face to Damas's sober expression and then she addressed Alexa. "I hope nothing's wrong. Your husband was in quite a hurry. He knew he could leave her safely with me. I was glad to be of help. The three of you make such a nice little family.''

Family! The word cut through Alexa with bitter irony.

''We appreciate your help,'' said Damas smoothly, and lifted the baby from her arms. Putting Dorrie's sleeping head on his shoulder, he patted her little fanny reassuringly.

''You're good with the little one—I can see that.'' Her smile broadened and she winked at Alexa. ''Looks like he has a way with women, all right.''

Alexa's smile was thin.

They walked back to their table and collected the diaper bag. Alexa slipped it over her shoulder, debating whether she should take Dorrie from him, and decided against it. The baby appeared angelic and contented in Damas's arms and she didn't want to deal with waking her up. There was little chance of getting away from her bodyguard in this isolated place.

''You didn't eat your lunch,'' Damas chided, nodding toward the box lunch.

''Neither did you.'' She pinned a level gaze on him. He was as taut as a tiger ready to spring. ''What's going on?''

''I'm not sure exactly. And I never indulge in speculation.''

A flash of anger crossed her face. ''You just do as you're told—is that it?''

He shrugged. ''Something like that.''

She grabbed his arm as he started to turn away. ''Liar! You're not a mindless robot. There's a decent streak in you a mile wide.''

He gave her a half smile. ''If you say so.''

Alexa's voice suddenly trembled with desperation. "Please, listen to me. I can't be here when Leo comes. He's going to get his revenge by taking the baby away. You know him…he'll do what he says. Can't you see? He'll hide Dorrie away until the courts give him total custody. Please, help me get away."

"I never get involved in domestic quarrels, Mrs. Santini," he said coldly. "A man would be a fool to get in the middle between you and Leo. Dorrie is his child … and you're his wife."

No, I'm not, she wanted to scream at him, but the set of his jaw told her she didn't dare. He was ruthless to the core. She'd been stupid trying to appeal to his better nature. His loyalty to Santini was unshaken. His tenderness for the baby had led her astray.

"Let's go. The other wagons are getting ready to go back. Have you had enough sight-seeing? That's why you came on this little jaunt, wasn't it?" The question dripped with sarcasm.

She lifted her chin slightly to meet his eyes. She wouldn't make the mistake of misjudging him again. He was a Santini man through and through. "I've seen all I want to."

They didn't speak on the way back. The tour consisted of a circle around the lake and Alexa was as jumpy as a cricket by the time they returned to the hotel. It was nearly midafternoon and time was running out.

Dorrie woke up and they gently put her back in the stroller when they reached the hotel. Alexa took hold of the handle and pushed her at a brisk pace down the sidewalk. She didn't need to look around to know that Damas was walking casually behind her.

She had no idea what to do next. They entered the lobby and she automatically headed for the elevator. Just as she reached it, the door swung open and Zurick's pretty brunette friend, Rhonda, stepped out.

"There you are, honey," she said in a slurred voice. "Frank's been trying to reach you...hic...we're having a party...and you're invited." She gave Alexa a sloppy smile and then turned to Damas. She stuck a wobbly finger on his chest. "And so are you, handsome." She clung to him as she wavered on her feet.

Alexa pushed the stroller past them into the elevator.

Rhonda gave a drunken giggle as she put her arms around Damas's neck. She began to sag, then her body went completely limp. Alexa watched from inside the elevator as Damas struggled to keep her from falling on the floor.

The elevator doors shut. With a reflex action, she never quite understood, Alexa pushed the garage-level button. As the elevator descended, she hurriedly took Dorrie out of the stroller, put the diaper bag on her shoulder and stepped out into the underground garage as soon as the door opened. Quickly she wedged the empty stroller in the door so it wouldn't shut. She gave a frantic glance around and spied the ramp leading to the outside.

She knew that the taxi station was just beyond the opening to the garage. She spun in that direction. There was a chance that she could make it outside and engage a taxi before Damas came after her.

She started toward the entrance at a run. The distance was much greater than she had expected. Dorrie protested against the strange hold and the bouncing run.

About halfway to the entrance, she saw a middle-aged couple putting suitcases into the trunk of a car.

"For heaven's sake, Millie. Hurry up. We're going to miss our plane. Just throw that beach bag somewhere and let's go." The man spoke in a thick Texas drawl as he slammed down the trunk lid and started toward the driver's seat. His wife took a few steps around the car and then stopped as Alexa hurried over to her.

"Pardon me," said Alexa. "I couldn't help hearing. I wonder...I wonder if you'd be so kind as to let me ride with you to the airport. My transportation is delayed—I'm afraid I'll miss my flight." She used her own professional voice and manner.

"Of course. Hop in. William will have us there in no time."

"Thank you. I really appreciate it."

The woman climbed in the front seat and her husband barely waited for Alexa to slam the back door, before he shoved the car into gear and roared out of the garage.

Alexa sat low in the seat until they had left the resort and were several miles down the highway. Her head was spinning, as if her fast, shallow breathing wasn't supplying enough oxygen. Nervous sweat beaded on her forehead and her stomach churned. She gave Dorrie her elephant to play with, leaned her head back against the seat and allowed the furious beating of her heart to ease.

Bless Rhonda, she thought, permitting herself a small, satisfied smile.

Chapter Twelve

The fifteen-mile ride into the resort town of Grandview took an excruciating eternity. Even though the man drove a few miles above the speed limit, it seemed to Alexa that a bicycle could have easily caught up with them. She kept looking out the back window. She wouldn't have been surprised to see Damas pull up in a car beside them any moment. Her only hope was that he would have his hands so full with Rhonda that he wouldn't realize right away that Alexa hadn't taken the elevator up to her suite. Once he realized that the elevator had gone down and hadn't come back up, he'd charge down into the garage and find the stroller wedged in the door.

He'd check the taxi station first, she speculated. When told that no woman with a baby had left the hotel in a taxi during the past few minutes, he might decide she was still in the garage. Of course, someone could have seen the couple's car leave the garage, but she had tried to keep out of sight until they had left the resort. Maybe someone had seen her running through the garage. Damas might find a witness who— *Stop it!* She jerked her thoughts away from fruitless speculation. *Take it a step at a time,* she lectured herself. She'd made it away from Foxfire. With luck she could get a commuter flight back to New York within the hour. It would take time to verify the passenger list and by then she should be airborne.

As they entered the outskirts of Grandview, a reassuring sign identified the airport exit. During the trip from the hotel, Alexa held Dorrie and put the seat belt around both of them. The baby slobbered happily and played with her teething ring. She probably needed her diaper changed and there was only one bottle left. The challenge of coping with a fussy baby on a plane with everyone sending glaring looks in her direction twisted her stomach with new anxiety. Dorrie seemed to sense her less-than-confident handling and Alexa prayed that she'd make it to New York without the baby creating more of a nightmare than the situation itself already did. She took a deep breath to still a rising tension that made every nerve in her body ready to snap. Handing Dorrie to Mia would make all the trouble worthwhile, she reminded herself.

"We'll let you out at the terminal before we turn in the rental car," said the husband, studying Alexa in the mirror. "You traveling alone?"

"No, I'm meeting someone," she lied. "My luggage has already gone ahead." She was astounded at how glib she'd become at falsehoods.

"What airline?"

Alexa hesitated. "Transair."

"Never heard of it."

"It's a small commuter line."

Alexa had taken Transair several times when attending education conferences in upstate New York.

She knew the company offered early-afternoon flights into Kennedy airport from several cities. She prayed Grandview was one of them.

Traffic into the airport was a snail's pace and Alexa worried her lower lip in a nervous gesture as they crept along. Cars were lined up in front of the terminal with people unloading baggage.

Making sure Mia's purse was in the diaper bag, she looped the bag over her shoulder and lifted the baby up in her arms. The minute the car stopped, she was out the door.

"Thank you," she said breathlessly.

"Have a nice trip, dearie," said the woman. Alexa slammed the back door and took off toward the building, joining a throng of people pushing through the terminal door. Inside, she was thrown off stride for a moment while she searched the long lobby for the Transair ticket counter. When she located it, she was relieved to find that there were only two travelers ahead of her and a flight was scheduled within the hour.

As she stood in line and waited, her eyes kept returning to the front doors. She prayed that Damas wouldn't be one of the people hurrying into the building.

"Next flight is at three-forty-five," a pretty ticket clerk told her.

Alexa pulled out Mia's credit card. She was getting more adept at forging her sister's handwriting, but the woman didn't even look on the back of the card to compare signatures.

"That flight will be loading in about twenty minutes. Concourse H."

Twenty minutes. Alexa took off for the nearest rest room. She would keep out of sight until the last minute, then hurry through the busy airport and climb aboard the plane.

Dorrie continued to be a little angel while Alexa dallied in the rest room and Alexa's heartbeat had about returned to normal when it was time to head for concourse H.

She had started down a long ramp that led to the security area, when she was struck dumb. Heading straight at her, coming up the concourse in a line of arriving travelers, was— It couldn't be! Her eyes had to be deceiving her—this nightmare couldn't be getting worse. But she recognized Leo Santini instantly from all the newspaper and television coverage he'd had. Thick iron gray hair, a wide-bridged nose, heavy cheeks and blunt jaw gave his face a hard, chiseled expression. He was flanked by two men in dark suits. She blinked again just to make certain that it was truly Leo and his henchmen walking straight toward her. She felt as if she were going to faint. Dorrie wiggled in her arms and she clutched the baby tighter.

If Santini saw her and the baby, he would take her for Mia. *But not for long.* He would surely detect the impersonation immediately. She couldn't just stand there and give up.

She spun around on her heel. Struggling with the baby and the dangling diaper bag, she fled back in the direction she had come. Every second she expected someone to call out to her, "Mia," or "Mrs. Santini."

By some miracle, she made it back to the main terminal ahead of his entourage. She headed for the sanctuary of the rest room, but never reached it. Coming toward her from the other direction was Malchek, his chauffeur's cap in hand. She couldn't go back or forward. If she remained where she was, she would be caught between Leo and Malchek.

She quickly turned into a small shop in the corridor selling books and magazines. The whole front of the store was open and a wrought-iron paperback rack was the only thing that offered slight concealment. As she stood behind it, she caught a glimpse of Malchek as he went by. If he had glanced in her direction, he would have seen her and the baby.

The minute he had passed, she went out into the corridor again. She kept her head down, huddled against the baby's. She had no idea how far the men were behind her and didn't dare turn around to see. Walking rapidly, she put as many people between herself and them as she could.

Thank heavens she knew where the rest room was. She bounded through the crowd walking in the same direction. She prayed she could make it around the corner without being seen.

Dorrie protested the rough, jostling gait. Arching her back, the baby stiffened and thrust her legs out in every direction.

"Oh, no, please, Dorrie...please not now," Alexa prayed.

The baby's cries gathered momentum, rising to screeching level with every intake of air. The diaper bag strap slipped off Alexa's shoulder and dangled heavily on her arm. She tried to get it back into position and manhandle the baby at the same time.

Somehow the Velcro fastening on a side pocket of the bag popped open and the pink elephant fell out.

Let it go.

Alexa didn't slow her hurried stride. She turned the corner, and a moment later someone fell into step beside her and once again a familiar hand held out the stuffed toy.

She couldn't turn her head. She kept walking, stunned, caught in total disbelief. It couldn't be. Not when she'd gotten this close. Her vision blurred with sudden tears. Disappointment and frustration became too great. Something inside her shattered. The will to resist went out of her. She surrendered to her utter defeat.

She must have wavered, for Damas put his arm firmly through hers and held her closely by his side.

"Easy does it," he said in clipped tones.

He guided her out of the terminal and hurried her into a taxi that had just deposited a fare in front of the terminal. He gave orders to the driver and then climbed in the back seat beside her.

Dorrie was still crying at the top of her lungs.

"Let me have her," he ordered, and she handed him the baby without protest. He put Dorrie over his shoulder and patted her bottom. "Give me the other bottle."

Alexa mechanically did as he directed. Once Dorrie had the nipple in her mouth, she quieted down immediately in his arms. Alexa couldn't bear to look at either of them. She let her head fall back against the cushion and closed her eyes, and a large tear slid down each cheek.

Defeat washed over her. *He's taking us back to Foxfire.* In a few minutes they would be back at the hotel. She doubted if anyone would know she'd been away. Her bodyguard had saved his neck by thwarting her escape. By a thin margin Leo Santini's wife would be at the resort when he arrived in the limo. Dorrie would be put back in Clara's hands and Leo would know that some stranger was pretending to be his wife. The plan to get the baby away from Mia's husband would become clear. She had probably made things worse for Mia by consenting to the wild scheme.

But it could have worked. She had almost pulled it off. Anger began to replace the numbness. She brushed the tears from her cheeks and turned her head to glare at Damas. He'd beaten her and she hated him. She despised him for hounding her steps, for sending her emotions into a tailspin every time he came near her. He played on her feelings, making her forget that he was nothing but one of Santini's hoods.

"How can you live with yourself?" she lashed out. "How can you do it?"

He looked over the baby's soft fair head at Alexa. "Do what?" he asked quietly.

"Act like you care about Dorrie and then hand her over to the likes of Santini. You know what kind of an upbringing she'll have with him. She deserves better and you know it."

He laid Dorrie on her tummy across his lap and patted her fanny, and after a gurgle of contentment, the baby went on sleeping. "It's not my choice."

"Yes, it is! You said you didn't want to get involved in any domestic fracas, but you *are* involved! You're right in the middle of it. You're stopping me from making the right decision . . . to leave Leo. Your interference is responsible for Dorrie's future and . . . mine." She'd almost said "Mia's." "Who gives you the right to destroy lives? That's what you're doing. Don't you have any feelings at all?"

The color drained from his face and a flash of blue firelike anger crossed his eyes. "On occasion."

"Please don't do this," she begged. "In your heart you know it isn't right."

He sighed. "Leading with my heart has never proven to be my strong suit. A lesson I should have learned. But I'm afraid I haven't."

She stared at him. "What do you mean?"

"Just what it sounds like. I've taken leave of my senses."

His gaze traveled over her tear-streaked face. "It's insanity to let you get to me the way you do." He reached over and gently wiped away a lingering tear with his fingertip. For a moment, they just looked at each other, caught in a wordless communication that expressed a bewildering well-spring of feelings.

He cupped her chin with his hand and searched her glistening blue eyes. "I'm not taking you back to Foxfire. I'm a fool, a damn fool."

She thought he was going to kiss her, but he didn't. He drew back and stared out the car window.

"You're doing the right thing."

He acted as if he hadn't heard her.

"Leo was at the airport . . . and Malchek was there to meet him. I guess you know that. Anyway, they'll be gone by now, so it will be safe to go back there."

"No," he said shortly. "Not safe at all. I'll have to make some arrangements."

"Arrangements? You don't have to make any arrangements. It's very simple. I already have an airline ticket on Transair, so I can catch their next scheduled flight to New York. If I'd been able to dodge Leo and Malchek—and you—at the airport, I'd be on my way back right now. Just take me back to the airport and—"

He looked at her in a humoring way. "Not a good idea."

"But why? The sooner I get away from here the better."

"It's not going to be that simple. When Leo gets to the hotel and finds out you've skipped, he'll have his men all over this airport, tracking down that ticket and your destination. While you're still in the air, he'll arrange a welcoming committee at the other end. The minute you and the baby step off that plane, you'll have a conducted tour back to him."

Alexa fell silent.

"I told you. I'll have to make some arrangements. The whole picture is going to be different now. When I saw the limo leave the hotel, I guessed Malchek was going to pick up Leo. And I was pretty sure that you'd managed to catch a ride to the airport. I wasn't certain that I wouldn't find you in the arms of your husband when I got there." He searched her face. "There's no turning back, you know, for either of us."

"What will Leo do...when he finds out you helped us?"

His jaw hardened. "You don't want to know."

If it hadn't been for the baby sleeping on his lap, she would have gone back to the hotel and faced Santini herself. She knew that Damas had put his own life in jeopardy. "What are we going to do?"

"You've got to let me handle everything. That means you've got to stay out of sight while I set things up. You've got to trust me."

Alexa gave him a weak smile. Trust? The word stabbed her conscience. How could she continue to live the lie? Should she tell him that he didn't have Leo Santini's wife on his hands, but an imposter. What would he do? The possible answer frightened her. Would he wash his hands of the whole business? Dump her out at Foxfire and leave her to explain the deceit? She bit her lip. No, she couldn't risk it. He was willing to help *Mia Santini* leave her husband. For the moment, that's all that mattered. She hated deceiving him, but she really didn't have any choice.

He handed the sleeping baby to Alexa, leaned forward and told the taxi driver to stop at the first telephone booth. The taxi pulled into a truck stop at the edge of an industrial area. Damas got out, crossed the parking lot and closed the doors of the booth before dialing. Alexa saw him gesture as he talked, as if trying to convince someone of something.

A quiver of fear slithered through Alexa's stomach. Who was he talking with? She had an uneasy feeling as she watched him through the glass windows. He made agitated movements with his head and shoulders as he listened to the person on the other end of the line. Had he been leading her on, making her believe that he was going to jeopardize his position with Santini to help her get away? Maybe he was making arrangements for her to be turned over to Leo. *Had he tricked her?*

The impulse to get out of the car and make a run for it was strong, but she knew from past failures that she'd never get very far. Her ineptitude at eluding him was painfully clear.

He came back to the car and gave the driver an address. The man turned the vehicle around and headed back into the center of Grandview.

At least they weren't heading toward Foxfire anymore, thought Alexa with a shiver of relief. "Where are we going?"

"To a boarding house."

She swallowed back a rising protest and in as neutral voice as she could manage she asked, "Why a boarding house?"

"It's a safe place to stay for the moment."

"But I have to get back to New York."

"Why? You running to someone who's going to take Guy's place?" The question held a sarcastic bitterness. He'd known all along that she gathered men like beads on a string, but the knowledge did nothing to stop him from falling for her. When it came right down to it, he didn't give a damn how many others there had been. He had to have her. He'd always laughed at guys who let some gal twist their guts into a pretzel, but he was as trapped as any of them. He was sacrificing his future—and maybe his life—because he couldn't do anything else.

"No. There's no one...like that."

"Then you'd better give up going back to the city for the time being," he snapped, knowing she was probably lying through her pretty white teeth.

"But I have to get back home as soon as possible," she protested.

His eyes flashed anger and his voice was hard. It was all he could do to keep his hands off that graceful neck of hers. "This isn't any harmless game we're playing. You'd damn well better do as I say, Mrs. Santini, or you'll have both our necks in a sling in quick order. Don't make me ask myself if you're worth it!"

She muffled her anxiety. He had told her to trust him. *What other choice do I have?*

The taxi stopped in front of a three-story Victorian house in a modest neighborhood. Damas paid the driver, took the baby and put a guiding hand on Alexa's arm as she wrestled with the diaper bag.

A spry redheaded landlady answered the door and acted as if arrangements had already been made. Damas must have made the call from the telephone booth, Alexa speculated as the woman escorted them up to the second floor, down a back hall to a spacious bedroom with a private bath.

What had Damas told her? Alexa noticed that the landlady didn't ask their name. Did she take them for a properly married couple with a baby daughter?

"I'll have my husband bring up a crib," she said in a friendly but detached manner. "And anything else you may be needing."

"Thank you, Mrs. O'Dell," Damas said. The ease with which Damas had just spoken made Alexa wonder if he'd been there before. He closed the door behind Mrs. O'Dell and turned to her.

"I know the accommodations are a comedown from what you're used to. Maybe you can put up with them for a short while."

Alexa wanted to laugh. The old-fashioned room was twice the size of her apartment bedroom. Compared with her postage-stamp bathroom, the adjoining one was pure luxury, with its deep claw-footed bathtub and marble sink. A lovely high bed with a crocheted bedspread and ruffled pillows put her furnishings to shame.

"Something funny?"

She sat down on the bed beside the sleeping baby. "I think the room is lovely. And I'm grateful to you."

He rammed an agitated hand through his hair. The lady was grateful. Good old Boy Scout Silva. Protector of womanhood. What a laugh. Hell, she'd turn and run out of the room if she knew he was within a heart's beat of stripping off her clothes and satisfying the explosive hunger eating away at him.

"How long do I have to stay here? The baby's out of bottles and—"

"I know. We'll need more formula and disposable diapers." He jerked his eyes away from the slinky pink jumpsuit molding her luscious body like a silk glove. "I'll see what I can do about a change of clothes for you."

"How long am I going to be here."

"As long as it takes."

"I don't understand—"

"Neither do I and I wish to hell I did. And don't ask me why I have lost my head over a married woman who pulls the strings of every man she meets."

"Damas, I . . ." Her voice was husky. The air between them like a tinderbox. A combustible heat waited for one touch, one word. "I'm not married," she said with a rush. She couldn't keep the truth from him any longer. Nothing seemed to matter at that moment but taking away all the barriers between them. "I'm not Mia Santini... I'm her twin sister."

Damas froze as if he'd turned into stone.

"It's true. I'm Alexa Widmire, a teacher at Hunter College. I pretended to be Mia so I could get Dorrie away from Leo."

"You're a liar," he growled. "You're making the whole thing up." Even as he shouted at her, the truth hit him like a crash of cymbals in his ears. All the clues had been there and he'd been so infatuated that he had missed every one of them. He'd been duped. Played for an utter fool.

"Please, understand..." she pleaded as she drew back from the fury exploding in his eyes.

"I understand, all right." He grabbed her by the shoulders and roughly pushed her back on the bed. She winced as his strong fingers bit into her flesh. He reaped some satisfaction from the terror that fled into her eyes.

"Do you know what you've done? You've just sabotaged my future. And what is worse, you've just wrecked months of undercover work."

Chapter Thirteen

Damas saw a flood of bewilderment cross her face.

"Undercover? I don't—"

He cut off her breath with an angry kiss that poured out his fury and pent-up frustration. He wanted to show her that she'd tricked the wrong guy. She'd turned him inside out once too often with her seductive soft mouth and smoky eyes. Feeling her supple body under his, he lost himself in the swell of wild sensation that threatened to drown him. He reached for the long zipper running down the front of her jumpsuit. She pushed against him in protest as the soft cloth fell away and exposed white breasts spilling out of wispy lace cups, and a sheer bikini circling her hips. He wanted to lose himself in the cradle of her loveliness, but something held him back. Her vulnerability mocked him. He couldn't take her like this. Not in anger and revenge. He closed the zipper and pushed himself away from her.

Sitting on the edge of the bed, he put his head in his hands. "You have no idea what you've done, do you? Months of planning and putting my butt on the line day after day—all for nothing!"

She slowly raised up and searched his face as she sat beside him. Her breathing was rapid and her voice husky. "Is it really true...that you're not...? She swallowed hard and said haltingly, "You mean...that you're an undercover agent?"

He nodded. "That's exactly what I am. There's going to be hell to pay."

"Yes," she murmured. She couldn't keep the relief out of her voice. *He wasn't a Santini henchman.*

"You don't get it, do you? You don't understand what's going on?"

"Yes, I do," she insisted quietly. There had been a revengeful passion in his ruthless kisses. "I'm not *me*...and you're not *you.*" More than anything in the world she wanted him to look at her as Alexa and not Mia. She ached for him to love her with a tenderness that was for her alone.

He got up and began to pace the room. After a few silent minutes, he pulled out a chair a safe distance from the bed, where she sat.

"All right. Let's have the whole story from the beginning. Everything! Santini is probably at the resort by now, wondering where his little wife has gone. I've got to make some sense out of the whole blasted thing before it's too late."

He saw her moisten her lips and straighten her back. "Start at the beginning."

When she began talking, her words were clear and precise. Before his eyes, she became a professional woman who knew how to handle herself. She seemed relieved that she no longer had to hold back, pretending to be what she wasn't. She told him about Mia's unexpected visit and her own visit to Guy's apartment to get the earrings.

"I saw you there," she said with a lift of her chin. "And I knew you had found the other earring. When I came back without it, Mia was afraid that Leo would know everything. She convinced me that we had to get the baby away from him while there was still time. The plan seemed simple. I was to go to her house, get Dorrie and take her to Mia so she could take the baby and leave him for good." Her eyes blazed at Damas. "Only, you ruined everything!"

"I can't believe you'd consent to such a hare-brained scheme," he countered. "Why on earth would you do it?"

"Because Mia is the only family I have. I just couldn't turn my back on her and the baby." Her lower lip quivered. "All my life I've wanted someone to really need me. I couldn't just stand back and let Santini destroy Mia and shut Dorrie away from her. They needed my help. I never dreamed that things would turn out the way they did."

He swore under his breath for being so stupid not to have tumbled to the impersonation. Looking back to that first moment when he had intercepted her hurrying away from the house, she hadn't been the kind of woman that he had expected. He should have trusted his instincts, instead of ignoring a nagging feeling that something wasn't right about her. For one thing, she didn't match her reputation. He'd had a dozen clues that she wasn't what she seemed and he had ignored them all. It rankled him to know that she had jerked his string every inch of the way.

"What is going to happen now?" she demanded, breaking the silence. She wanted to ask him a hundred questions about his personal life and his job, but his stony expression stopped her. His eyes narrowed with a flinty hardness as he looked at her.

"I'll have to get back to the department before I can answer that," he replied curtly. "My supervisor okayed this safe house for Mia Santini and her baby. My instructions were to leave you, get myself back to Foxfire and let the department handle all the necessary security measures to safely transport you and the baby away from here."

"But you can't go back to the hotel...."

He stood up and strode to the door. "I've got to make some telephone calls. You stay here." He sent her a fierce scowl. "I mean it. You've done more than enough damage already."

"WHAT IN THE HELL are you trying to tell me?" barked Captain Talbot.

The roar in Talbot's voice sent Damas's ears ringing. "You heard me. The gal I thought was Mia Santini is her twin sister. The two of them hatched some plan to get Mia's baby out of Santini's clutches. She's been trying to steal the baby out from under my nose," Damas said bitterly, "I've been guarding the wrong woman."

"Let me get this straight. You had me make arrangements to get Leo Santini's wife into a safe house. Only, she's not his wife. She's not the mother of his baby. She's an imposter. Is that right?"

Damas grunted.

"She had no legal grounds, right? She's taken the baby under false pretenses. And we've got this would-be kidnapper set up in a safe house, right?"

"Yes, but—"

"Get her out of there. Now! Of all the stupid messes! We can't get involved. Let her fend for herself. Maybe we can salvage your undercover work after all. Tell Santini you suspected something and have been following it up. Use the situation to get back in his good graces. We're too close to nailing the guy to drop the ball now. He'll thank you for uncovering the deceit. You—"

"No," he said. "I can't do that. Santini will eat her alive."

"You aren't hearing me, Silva. Get out of the safe house and get your butt back to Foxfire—and take her with you! That's an order." Talbot punctuated the command by slamming down the receiver.

Damas hung up and stared at the phone. He'd joined the police force when he was hardly more than a gawky, eager kid. Through study and determination he had worked himself up through the ranks. When he had been chosen fifteen months ago for the Santini undercover job, he had accepted the assignment as a kind of graduation diploma. He hadn't been prepared for the ugly demands that would be made upon him. He'd done what he had to do to stay in Santini's good graces . . . even to killing a man. Dumping a deceitful, conniving woman should be easy.

ALEXA WAS in the downstairs hall, just hanging up the telephone, when he came in. His expression was as dark as a mine pit and she felt her stomach tighten.

"Who were you talking to?" he demanded.

"My sister ... I had to let her know what's happening. She's beside herself with worry. I've got a neighbor staying with her. I'm afraid Mia may do something foolish. I tried to reassure her, but I couldn't tell her how long we'd be staying here."

"About fifteen minutes," he answered gruffly, and urged her up the steps. Her hips brushed his as she moved closely at his side and he was aware of the rhythmic grace of her legs and hips. Her rounded fanny danced under the smooth ripple of the pink jumpsuit. "Get your things together. We're leaving."

"What's wrong? You said—"

"I know what I said." He didn't look at her as they entered the bedroom. "Things have changed. You can't stay here."

His abruptness dispelled any notion of protection she'd had. She felt like someone who had been offered a life preserver, only to have it grasped out of her drowning hands. The baby was peacefully sleeping in the crib that Mrs. O'Dell had sent up earlier with her grandson. Alexa had enjoyed a few minutes of normalcy as she'd chatted with the gangly teenager. She had always related well to young people and some of her confidence had come back. She'd walked downstairs with him and called Mia. She'd told her sister that now someone was going to help her ... the worst was over.

"Thank God," Mia had sobbed. "Please bring my baby to me."

"I will. Soon," Alexa had promised. Damas had come in at that moment and wiped out her rising optimism with one black look.

"Why do we have to leave?" she demanded as she watched him grab up the diaper bag. "What's happening? Didn't you say we'd stay here until you could arrange something?"

"That's when I thought I had Mia Santini and her baby daughter to safeguard." He refused to meet her eyes. "My superior doesn't take to the idea of aiding and abetting a kidnapper. And I can't say I'm crazy about the idea myself."

I shouldn't have told him. The impulse to be honest with him had brought disaster. She'd let her emotions run away with her and had trusted the undeniable sexual current that sparked between them. Not only had he cruelly rejected her, but he wanted to get her off his hands as quickly as possible. Was he preparing to take her back to Foxfire?

She moved in front of him, forcing him to meet her steely gaze. "I deserve to know. Are you turning me over to Santini?"

"There's no time to talk about it now. Let's go." He picked up the baby and tossed Alexa the diaper bag.

She wanted to protest, yet she had no choice but to do as he said. As long as he had the baby, she was restrained from any rebellion as effectively as if he'd put handcuffs on her. She followed him down the stairs and out the front door.

The day had turned gray and wet. A light rain glistened on the trees and pavement. A quickening breeze warned that benign sprinkles would soon turn into a downpour. A late-model Plymouth sedan was parked at the curb and she glimpsed rental license plates as he opened the door for her. She glanced in the back seat and her eyes widened with surprise. Boxes of diapers, bottles, baby formula, blankets, and several grocery and department store sacks were piled next to a baby's car seat. He'd been shopping and the car was packed for traveling.

He put the baby in the car seat, slammed the door and climbed into the driver's side. She sat in the front seat beside him, staring at his rigid profile, trying to understand this stranger.

He gunned the car away from the safe house, leaning slightly forward in the seat as windshield wipers swept increasing rain splatters away. He turned onto an interstate running north.

The opposite direction from Foxfire.

"You're not taking us back?"

He gave a short nod. "That's right."

"Why not?"

His hands tightened on the steering wheel. "Can't you guess?" He gave a self-deprecating laugh. "I've taken utter leave of my senses. Gone stark raving mad. Decided to disobey my superior's orders. Put myself at risk from both Santini and the law. Not what you would call rational thinking by any means."

"But what about your undercover work?"

"Shot to hell. Down the drain. Kaput!"

"Surely you can explain the situation to someone," she protested, suddenly sick to her stomach. Damas's career was on the line—and it was her fault. "There must be something you can do."

"I have bent my superior's ear into a cauliflower, but as far as he is concerned, the facts add up to one thing. You are *not* Mia Santini and you have no right to be taking the baby from her father. This is child snatching. Plain and simple. You are engaged in

kidnapping and so is anyone else who gets involved . . . namely yours truly.''

''No, I can't let you. She moved closer to him. Her
hand tingled as she fought an impulse to lay it on his
muscular leg. She was afraid of another physical rejection.

''It's too late. It's already done. Now we're in the
same boat. I guess I'll find out how it feels to be outside the law. I'm not sure I could have salvaged anything by exposing you to Leo anyway. I'm pretty sure
he set me up to get more damaging evidence on Mia.
Malchek was watching our every move and we were
pretty obliging when it came to giving him fuel for his
report.''

''We didn't do anything,'' she declared.

He gave her a wry smile. ''Only because the water
was too muddy to see clearly what was happening to
us.''

''And what was happening?'' she challenged. Her
heartbeat quickened. His abrupt denial of the passion that had sprung between them had left her shaken
and uncertain. She wanted to hear him admit that the
explosive attraction between them was valid.

He reached over and took her hand without answering her question. She debated giving him a taste
of rejection by withdrawing her hand from his, but
decided against it.

''Where are we going?''

''It depends. I thought we'd take a circular route
back to the city. Cross the Delaware before heading
south, but something's bothering me. That call you
made to your sister today. Was it the first one?''

Alexa shook her head. "No, I called her a couple of times from the hotel."

"From the suite?"

She nodded.

He swore and took an off ramp to a nearby service station. For a minute, she thought he was going to turn around and head back. "Why? What's the matter."

"Don't you know hotels keep a record of telephone calls placed from each room?"

"I . . . I never thought about it."

"When Santini tumbles to the fact that you're gone, he's going to check any calls made to or from your room. And guess where that's going to lead him? Right smack to your apartment."

She caught her breath. "Then he'll know everything."

"Even if Mia doesn't answer the phone, he'll send someone around to check the place out. She's got to get out of there . . . now!"

"But where can she go? She can't walk without help."

"Have you got any friends close by who could come and get her? Hide her out until we get there?"

The answer was no. Never had Alexa felt so depleted of friendship. She couldn't think of anyone willing to be drawn into such a sordid mess. "I don't have any close friends," she admitted in a choked voice.

"What about relatives?"

"My adoptive parents are retired. They're in England at the moment." *Who could she call?* The question played like a broken record in her mind. No one at the college. The only person in the apartment house she really knew was Mrs. Trimble.

"That's it!" She turned to Damas. "The neighbor who's looking after Mia has a cottage in Maine. She was planning on leaving this weekend for her summer vacation. I bet she would take Mia with her if I explained the situation."

"Good." He took the baby from her and nodded toward the telephone booth at the front of the station. "Use the pay phone. Tell Mrs. Trimble to get Mia out of there now. Tell them not to answer the phone for any reason and to leave by the back door. Be sure and find out exactly where this Trimble place is so we can meet them there."

A blast of wind and rain hit Alexa in the face as she dashed from the car into the station. There was no question in her mind about doing exactly as Damas had ordered. He knew what they were up against.

Trying to convince Mia wasn't easy. "Damas Silva is going to help us. He's really an undercover agent and—"

"No, no, it's a trick. I don't care what he says." Mia's sobs rose. "He's one of Leo's men," she shrieked. "Don't let him take my baby."

"Mia, listen to me. I promise you that Dorrie is safe with him. Now, we've got to get you out of my apartment. The hotel has a record of the calls I made to you. If Leo checks, he'll have my number and will call it. Don't answer the phone. Understand? Don't answer the phone!"

A muffled sob was her only answer.

"Mia! For heaven's sake, grow up!" Alexa thought about the sacrifice that Damas was making and her patience snapped. "You're not the only one who has something to lose if this thing blows up in our faces. It's time you appreciated the awful mess you've gotten us into. Put Mrs. Trimble on the phone and then do exactly as she says."

Fortunately the older woman accepted the need for quick action and promised that she'd have Mia in the car within minutes. "I'm all packed and the car's been serviced. Don't worry about your sister. I'll have her safe and sound in my little retreat without anyone the wiser." She told Alexa where the cabin her husband had built was located in Bar Harbor.

"Thank you, Mrs. Trimble. You're a wonder. I know this is a real imposition...."

"Nonsense. I enjoy a little excitement now and then," she said in her practical tone. "Keeps me young. You take care, now, and bring that baby safely back to her mother, hear?"

Alexa was wet and shivering by the time she made it back to car. Dorrie was awake, stuffing her fists in her mouth.

"I think she's trying to tell us something," Damas said, still holding the baby. Her sucking sounds grew louder and her indignant cries rose above the steady downpour of rain.

He thrust the disgruntled infant into Alexa's arms and then quickly put the car back on the highway. Mia's warning lingered in Alexa's ears. *It's a trick. He's one of Leo's men.* How did she know he was telling her the truth? All this could be an elaborate ruse to make him look good with his boss. Maybe he was taking her to some rendezvous set up by Santini.

He'd flushed Mia out of her apartment, sent her out on the highway with Mrs. Trimble, where the two women could be easily overtaken. Had she dispatched them to an arranged accident?

She gave a muffled cry, which was drowned out by Dorrie's protesting bellows. Alexa turned and looked out the back window, but rain obscured her view. She couldn't be sure that the limousine, with Malchek at the wheel, wasn't following at a discreet distance. Apprehension built like pressure in a corked bottle, and she searched Damas's face. She saw that his jaw was clenched and his eyebrows almost matted together in a frown. That could mean anything. *Easy*, she told herself. She needed to stay calm, alert. Letting her imagination whip her into a frenzy would make her less able to handle the situation.

"What happens now?" she demanded, glaring at him.

Her hostile tone surprised him and he shot her a quick look. "Find a place to stop. An out-of-the-way motel."

"And you have one all picked out, of course."

He raised an eyebrow at her acidic tone and didn't answer. Driving in the downpour demanded total concentration. Every time a car went by in the other lane, water covered the windshield like spray from an open faucet. She couldn't see anything through her side window but murky shapes of trees and an occasional building as dark shadows of evening began to gather.

"I'd hoped to put more distance between us and Santini," he said finally in a loud voice to compete with Dorrie. "But it can't be helped. We can't keep going. We'll have to stop and take care of the baby."

By the time he pulled up in front of a small hotel that was set back from the highway, Alexa's nerves were like a frayed rope. She just wanted to be out of the rain and for the baby to stop crying.

The Shady Rest Motel, which Damas had chosen, was a small single-line unit that had seen better days. One electric light over a fading Vacancy sign was dim. In the assault of gray sheets of rain, the motel's dirty stucco exterior looked ready to crumble. Certainly not the kind of place that Mia Santini was likely to choose, no matter how desperate, Alexa thought. And not a likely spot for a rendezvous with Leo Santini.

Dorrie screamed the whole time that Damas was in the small office. Alexa took the baby out of the car seat and shifted her from one position to another. Her arms were aching by the time Damas came back, carrying a portable crib, and drove to the end unit.

He got out and unlocked the door. Holding a blanket over the baby's face, Alexa bolted from the car into the small L-shaped motel room.

Faded draperies matched an even more faded bedspread on a double bed. The floor slanted and the tiles in the bathroom were cracked. An old refrigerator in a tiny pantry kitchen made noises like some beast's disgruntled stomach.

Outside, lightning and thunder marched across the sky like an invading battalion. A forked spear of electricity hit somewhere in the nearby woods and a rebounding boom shook the walls of the cabinlike room.

Damas brought in all the stuff from the car and piled it on a rickety table, while Alexa walked the floor with Dorrie. He tossed a package of diapers on the bed. Alexa took the cue and began to wrestle out a dry one.

With purposeful speed, Damas put on a bent pan full of water to boil on a dirty, crusted stove burner. He placed a sterile disposable plastic liner in one of the new bottles and opened the package of formula. Using an enclosed measuring spoon, he put the correct amount of formula into the bottle and added the boiled water. He held the bottle under some cold running water for a minute and then sprinkled a few drops of formula on his inside wrist.

She watched him with a pang of longing that was as close to heartbreak as she ever wanted to feel. She'd never find another like him. She would never forget his courage and caring—and he would never forget her deceit.

"That should do it," he said, handing her the warm bottle.

When she put it into Dorrie's wide-open mouth, the baby choked on the flowing milk before she settled down to a greedy rhythmic sucking. In contentment, Dorrie slowly closed her eyes and her lashes made a delicate fringe on her pink cheeks. Alexa touched her lips to the baby's warm, soft forehead and felt her heart expand almost to the breaking point.

Damas kept glancing at them as he set up the portable crib. He saw Alexa tenderly kiss the baby and stroke her wispy blond hair. The picture was enough to make any man step in front of a firing squad, he thought grimly—if it came to that.

Dorrie fell sound asleep soon after finishing the bottle and Alexa put her down in the crib, just around a corner from the one large bed.

"She should sleep well for awhile," said Damas with satisfaction. "We'll have to boil some water to take with us. Then we can make up bottles as we need them. She'll be fine. Kids are adaptable, you know."

No, Alexa didn't know. And she didn't care. A bone-deep weariness swept over her. Wet hair clung to her head and lay limp on her neck. Her makeup had been smeared or wiped off altogether. Mia's fashionable pink jumpsuit was wrinkled and soiled, and smelled of Dorrie's dribbling. Everything about her was horrible and she felt totally demoralized.

She hated herself. She hated Mia. Most of all she hated this man who touched a deep reservoir of desire she hadn't known existed. Just being with him put a never-ending ache in her heart. There wasn't a damn thing she could do now to change anything between them. It had been too late from the moment they had met. She fought back tears as Damas's measuring gaze traveled over her.

He cursed himself when he saw the shadows in her eyes, the tired droop of her mouth and the brimming fullness in the corner of her eyes. "Come here." He held out his arms and pulled her close.

She wrapped her arms around his waist and for a brief moment gave in to the wonderful warmth of his protective embrace. He buried his face in her tousled hair and they stayed together without speaking for a long time.

Then he lifted her up in his arms and gently laid her down on the bed. When she looked up into his face, she saw that his dark eyes were luminous with a light that she had never seen before.

Chapter Fourteen

Tenderly and purposefully he removed her clothing, piece by piece. He drew off the lacy bra, and her rosy nipples rose as he brushed them with his thumb. Lowering his head, he caught a rising peak in his mouth and teased it with his flicking tongue, bringing a murmur of pleasure from her lips.

With seductive hands he peeled down the bikini briefs and let his strong long fingers stroke the smooth contours of her thighs and legs. She had never felt such arousing caresses and her whole body pulsated with voluptuous sensations.

He drew away and returned in a moment with a basin of warm water, cloth and towel. With tantalizing deliberateness he gently washed her and laid kisses on the tingling and prickling clean skin.

"Perfect," he murmured as his hands touched and molded her body. "Perfect."

Pleasure swept over Alexa, wave after wave, mounting with excruciating desire as his touch tuned her body to a vibrating pitch.

"Wait for me, love."

He left her again and she heard water running. When he returned, his nude body was moist and warm from a fleeting shower. As he slipped onto the bed beside her, she turned and curled eagerly against him. They began to explore each other, slowly, tenderly, then with a growing eagerness. He made her feel so special. His lovemaking was possessive, yet giving. Even as he delighted in her lips, throat and breasts, his body was not a separate entity from hers.

She whispered his name in delight and surprise when his hand slipped to the soft mound of her desire and with stroking fingertips sent her reeling to the edge.

"I'll catch you," he promised. When he swept her legs apart, he took her with command, and she was enveloped in an emotional and physical sharing that held nothing back.

Like a wild surf, rising and falling, they came together, taking, giving.

And when they lay quiet and content in each other's arms, Alexa rested her head in the hollow of his shoulder. Damas let his hand cup the warmth of her breast and put his leg across hers to hold her firmly at his side. "Go to sleep," he whispered, and brushed her cheek with a kiss.

The woman in his arms had claimed him on every level and the experience had shaken him. She had commanded total surrender of his mind, body and spirit—and he had willingly given it. No woman had ever had that effect on him. And her life was in his hands. He groaned and tightened his arms around her.

She stirred. "What is it?"

His voice was edgy. "I honestly don't know. Santini has eyes and ears in countless towns, police departments and state governments. He'll put out the word that Mia has taken his kid and run off with her bodyguard. Our descriptions will trickle down from a high official to paid informants living on the street.'' He didn't add that no matter where they went, the odds were great that someone could connect them with the missing baby.

She raised her hand and touched his cheek in a reassuring caress. "We'll be all right. Luck has been with us so far. Once we deliver Dorrie to her mother, the two of them can be put into safe custody, can't they?"

He nodded. A restraining order could be issued against Santini and a court battle for the child begun. There were no guarantees that Mia would win custody. She was up against powerful corruption that often permeated the justice system. Not all judges were above bribery and undue influence. They could only hope for the best.

Alexa snuggled closer to him and brushed a kiss over his bare chest. After a few minutes, her relaxed breathing told him she had fallen asleep. The trust she had in him made him all the more anxious. He knew better than to rely on luck. Santini was a ruthless man. He was vindictive and cruel when he was crossed. Nobody made a fool out of Leo Santini. No one.

Rain continued to pound the roof as he lay wideawake, staring at the ceiling. Alexa sighed peacefully in her sleep. He didn't know how in the hell he was going to keep her safe. In a few hours they would be on the run again. Somehow they had to make it to Mrs. Trimble's place without their scent being picked up by Santini's wolf pack. If Santini managed to in-

tercept them— Damas jerked his thoughts away from
the all-too-distinct possibility. He'd learned the hard
way that nothing ever went down as planned. Despite
the most diligent preparation, disaster could arrive
with a blink of an eye.

He finally dozed off an hour later, and fell into a
deep-enough sleep for his subconscious to betray him.
He was back in the warehouse again.

*Waiting. Dust in his nostrils. Darkness shattered
in a blaze of fire gunfire. Too late! Too late!
Groans, blood and death. McCalley twitched
until the second bullet. Bruno grinned and gave
Damas an arrogant wink. Then Bruno's grin was
gone—and his face with it.*

Damas lurched up bed.

Alexa gave a muffled protest and then came fully
awake with a start. "What is it?"

He was sitting straight up. A strangled groan came
from his heaving chest and he was covered in hot
sweat. At first she thought something in the room had
caused his violent reaction. It took a moment to realize he'd just come out of a nightmare. She put her
arms around him. He was stiff and unyielding. Every
muscle was as taut as a bowline, ready to snap.

She could see his pained expression because they
had left the bathroom light on and the door half-
closed to provide a night-light. He clenched his teeth
as though holding back a wrenching cry. Suddenly he
blinked and shuddered, as if the curtain of sleep had
parted, leaving him abandoned for a brief second in a
bewildering consciousness.

"You were dreaming…. It's all right," she soothed, stroking his cheek and turning his face toward hers. "It's all right."

His clouded eyes searched her face. He seemed startled to find her there beside him.

She tried to orient him. "Dorrie's asleep. The rain's stopped. And this miserable bed has enough lumps in it to give anyone a nightmare."

He drew an uncertain breath. "Sorry."

"Nothing to be sorry about. Come on, lie back down." She coaxed him onto the pillow beside her. He lay rigid for a long time, staring at the ceiling. With a deep intake of breath he turned on his side and drew her into the cup of his body. His arms tightened around her and he pressed his face into her soft neck. She felt his warm breath and the touch of his lips tasting her skin. He groaned like someone enduring unbearable thoughts.

"Want to tell me about it?" she asked gently.

He didn't answer for a long moment. Then he said gruffly, "You don't want to know."

"Yes, I do." Mia had already told her that he'd killed a police officer. "I have to know."

She thought he was going to ignore her, but when he began talking it was as if some release button had been pushed. He told her that he'd been undercover in the Santini organization about six months, when Leo had arranged for a drug delivery and had ordered him and an obnoxious creep named Bruno to be at a deserted warehouse to receive it. There hadn't been time for Damas to get word to the department through regular channels, but he'd managed to make contact with a rookie cop, McCalley, near the warehouse district.

Damas had told McCalley to pass the message along that something was going down.

Damas's voice thickened. "My mistake. The guy failed to get the information to the right people in time. The heroic fool showed up at the warehouse alone. Bruno and I were on the second floor, waiting for the dealers to come down through a trapdoor in the roof. Suddenly there was somebody below. Bruno heard him on the stairs. He swung around and fired."

A shudder went through Damas. "There was a horrible cry. The sound of a body falling back down the stairs. I knew who it was even before Bruno danced a flashlight over him. McCalley was no more than twenty-two. Just a freckled-faced kid. If I hadn't involved him, he'd still be alive."

"It wasn't your fault." *Damas hadn't shot him!* Tears of relief flooded her eyes. "You couldn't foresee what would happen."

"Bruno started grinning as he stood over the body. I picked up McCalley's gun and shot off Bruno's face while he was still laughing."

"What did you do then?" Her chest tightened as she just thought about the situation he'd been in.

"The shot scared the dealers off. I convinced Santini that McCalley had shot Bruno and I had killed the cop. Word got around that I was a cop killer. Put me in good with Santini. The FBI encouraged me to stick to the lie. I've had McCalley's blood on my hands ever since. I keep dreaming the whole thing over and over again."

She turned to face him and smoothed back the mussed hair from his forehead. She pressed her lips against his flushed brow.

He gave a deep groan. "And now I've fouled up again. God knows how this is going to turn out. If Santini gets his hands on either of us—"

"He won't," said Alexa with more confidence that she felt. She laid a path of light kisses to his rigid mouth. Under the pressure of her tugging lips and questing tongue, his mouth opened and captured hers. She slipped her hands down his back and locked him tightly against the cradle of her femininity. His physical response was immediate and they found each other again.

JUST BEFORE DAWN Dorrie woke them up with an indignant yell. Alexa groaned. Babies should have snooze buttons, she thought as she grabbed a pillow and put it over her head.

"No, you don't! Our little darling is calling." Damas jerked off the pillow. "Up and at 'em, sweetheart."

Alexa groaned. "Why don't you...?"

Damas laughed and pulled back the covers. "Nice try. Come on, I'll show you how to give a baby a bath."

Pure fright swept up into her face. She'd had a hard time holding on to a dry Dorrie. She could imagine what would happen if she was wet and slippery. "A bath?"

"She'll also need her diaper changed and a bottle." He gave her a grin. "Ladies' choice."

"Bottle," Alexa answered in a weak voice.

There was no sign of the rigid and tortured man who had trembled in her arms. He moved purposefully about the small room, orchestrating the feeding and bathing of the baby. He set a towel in the small cracked sink and filled it with warm water.

"Come on, princess." He eased Dorrie's rounded behind down into the water. A surprised look crossed her plump little face as she tentatively touched the water. A moment later she was giggling and splashing with delight. A softness crossed Damas's face as he bathed the baby.

Alexa's chest tightened. How could one man have so many facets? "Where did you learn to handle babies like this?"

"Plenty of practice. We lived in a place almost like this when my two youngest sisters were babies. Dad was out of work and my mother was sick, and I dropped out of school to help."

"But you went back to school?"

He nodded. "After a few months. It was hard to catch up, but I knew then what I wanted to do, and the police academy didn't take dropouts."

He handed a dried Dorrie into her arms. "I thought nothing meant as much to me as my career."

Her chest constricted with guilt. "I'm sorry. I wish I could undo everything."

"Everything?"

He leaned over the wiggling baby and kissed Alexa with a lingering, possessive pulling of her lips that sent warmth spiraling through her. When he drew back, he just looked at her solemnly for a long moment.

What was he thinking? Did he hate her for arousing him at every touch? Was he angrily fighting a desire to take her to bed again? His eyes were unreadable as he turned away and became all business again.

"I bought a few changes of clothes for the baby and one for you. Let's get on the road as quickly as we can." His jaw tightened.

She knew that he was right, but the ugly little motel room had become a halcyon retreat. For a foolish moment, she wished they didn't have to leave. She'd found a happiness in the hours they'd spent there that could be lost as quickly as it had come.

"Get dressed. I'll be back in a minute."

He went out the door and strode quickly to the far end of the motel unit, where an outside telephone booth stood near the access road. The air was heavy with moisture and swaths of gray clouds hung low. It would probably be noon before the sun broke through to burn off the haze, he thought. He wondered how the back roads would be after last night's downpour.

He slammed the door of the booth shut and quickly shoved a coin into the slot. When he got his number, he barked, "Get me Captain Talbot. Silva reporting."

Talbot answered the phone in a yell. "Damas! Where in the hell are you?"

"China."

Talbot let go with a string of swearwords. "You put your butt in a sling this time. You had your orders—"

"I didn't like them."

"Oh, you didn't like them. I'm so very sorry," Talbot said in a falsetto. Then his tone changed back to a cursing bellow. "You blasted fool! Santini's got his hounds out all over the place. You and that chick have bought into trouble, big time. You'd better come in *now*. Use your head. If Santini charges you as a kidnapper, you'll have your own men after you!''

Damas cut him off in the middle of a swearword. "Shut up and listen. You said the department could offer protection to Santini's wife—''

"His wife! Not some look-alike sister!''

"All right. I'm going to tell you where Mia Santini really is. I'm not sure how soon her husband will pick up her trail. I want you to get some men there right away. Keep her under protection until we arrive with the baby. Once we put the child into her hands, the courts will have to decide what to do about custody.'' He gave the directions to Mrs. Trimble's summer cabin at Bar Harbor, Maine.

"And when may we expect you and the pretend Mrs. Santini to appear?'' Talbot asked sarcastically. "Assuming, of course, that you two intend to show up at all.''

"Cut the crap, Talbot. We'll be there. Now listen. Here's the sister's address. That's where Mia Santini was staying while her sister went after the baby.'' He told Talbot about the calls Alexa had made from the hotel.

"Not too smart, is she?'' he taunted.

Damas ignored the snide jab. "If Santini's men are nosing around her place, they may beat you to Mia, so get on it!'' Damas hung up before Talbot could bellow that he was the one who was giving the orders.

Damas remained in the booth after he had hung up. He looked through the windows at the road that led back to the highway. An old pickup truck rumbled by and Damas instinctively kept his back turned until it had passed. He heard a door slam as someone came out of the office. A hefty woman moved down a narrow sidewalk, pushing a cleaning cart in front of her. She stopped at the first unit, knocked, then disappeared inside.

Damas left the booth. He hurried past the open door of the unit where the cleaning lady was vacuuming. There were only two other cars parked in front of motel rooms. Both vehicles were at least ten years old and his new rental car looked misplaced. In the crummy surroundings, anyone would probably notice it.

He was surprised to find Alexa holding a sleeping baby. She'd put everything he had bought back in grocery sacks and the baby paraphernalia was assembled in neat piles.

Alexa stood up, looking trim and seductive in the boy's jeans and checkered shirt he had purchased. She had pulled the front part of her hair back from her face and fastened it with a rubber band. Her face was devoid of makeup and her lovely eyes seemed larger than ever.

"Are we ready?"

He entertained a moment of cowardice. He knew too well the brutal life-style of the mob—no quarter given, no half measures and no excuses for failure. He also knew Santini's tenacity, his uncompromising pride. Could he keep her safe? She looked at him steadily and he gained courage from her quiet strength.

"Yes, ready," he said.

Chapter Fifteen

Alexa slipped Dorrie into the car seat while Damas quickly put everything but the diaper bag into the trunk. The fat cleaning lady was standing in the doorway of an empty unit when they left and he realized that she had probably been watching them load the car. *Don't get paranoid,* he told himself. The chances of Santini's men looking for them in this exact spot were unlikely. He knew that lookouts would be stationed at control points such as bridges and toll roads. Somehow they had to make their way through three states without detection. He decided they'd continue north until they could cross over into Vermont, then go across New Hampshire and into Maine. If Santini tumbled to the fact that they were headed for Bar Harbor, he could move his chess pieces to checkmate them at every point. Maybe luck would be on their side. Again—maybe it wouldn't.

DAMAS LEARNED LATER that it took only a few hours for Santini to find out that his wife, baby and bodyguard had spent the night at the Shady Rest Motel. Damas wasn't the least surprised when he heard that the owners, Lanky Harold and Big Bev, had a better source of income than the run-down motel. For three years the unit next to their living quarters had been used for drug trafficking in the area. Exactly what Damas had feared had happened. One of their early customers that morning had been Tony Petroni, a pusher who always spent a little time chitchatting with Harold and Bev.

They talked about the establishment that provided them with the goods of their trade and eventually the conversation came around to the Santini organization.

"The word's out," said Petroni. "Santini's wife is at it again. Run off with her new bodyguard and took the kid with her. The last dude ended up in the East River. Stone drunk. Drove his car right off the pier." He laughed. "Santini's boys always do a nice job. This new bodyguard must be as stupid as she is. The word is that there's big bucks for anyone who gets a line on them."

Bev's double chin worked up and down as she chewed on a chocolate-covered doughnut. "How old's the kid."

"A baby. Four or five months."

"And the fellow? What does he look like?"

"I think I saw him once in Albany," said Petroni, his thin face lined with a scowl. "He was with Santini. Somebody pointed him out. Dark hair, good build. Handsome quail bait. Killed a law officer when a buy went sour, so they say. I can't imagine him being stupid enough to buzz the boss's wife."

Bev licked her fingers thoughtfully. "Is she blond and skinny?"

Petroni smiled. Next to Bev a Green Bay Packers guard would be skinny. "A real looker, I hear. The Marilyn Monroe type."

"They were here. Unit ten. Left about seven this morning."

Her husband was already into his second gin for the day and he blinked at her stupidly. "What?"

Tony Petroni's dark eyes snapped. "You're kidding."

"Nope, I saw them leave. Harold checked them in last night. Did you have them sign the book?" she demanded of her blurry-eyed husband. It was obvious from his befuddled expression that he didn't remember.

"Get it," ordered Petroni.

There were no signatures for any of the three units that had been rented. Not a single license-plate number, either. Harold had taken the money and nothing else.

"What did the car look like?" Petroni asked Bev.

"New gray sedan... and I think it was a rental."

"Did you see what direction they went?"

"Didn't take the interstate. I thought it was funny at the time. Turned east on the county road." She grabbed Petroni's arm as he started to leave. "Big bucks, you said." Her puffy eyelids narrowed.

"I was exaggerating. Maybe a hundred or two. You'll get yours, Bev," he assured her. "I gotta pass along the info pronto." He glanced at his watch. "They've already been on the road a couple of hours."

DAMAS SWORE. The county road had been a grave mistake. Its gravel surface was like a washboard, causing the car to vibrate even at a cautious speed. Deep ruts had filled with water and the tires found little traction on the patches of mud. It was impossible not to lose vital time. If he tried to speed up the car might slip off the road and get mired like a mud turtle.

"We'll have to go back to the main highway." His mind raced. They had to change cars. He could expect Santini to check car rentals, and in the age of computers, he would know exactly what Damas was driving. "How much money do you have on you?"

She told him.

"Great. Forty-five dollars. We should be able to go a long way on that."

"I have Mia's credit cards. I could use her Plus card to get money."

"And leave a record that would pinpoint exactly where we are?"

She felt stupid. "I hadn't thought about that. What are we going to do?"

He didn't answer. They sat in silence for several minutes and then she held up her left hand. "Mia's wedding rings? They should be worth something ... if we could find a pawnshop."

He thought for a moment and then rewarded her with a nod. "Good idea. Better than drawing money from a bank. Most pawnbrokers keep their curiosity in check."

Damas turned back onto the main highway at the first opportunity. When road signs indicated that they were approaching a town, he took an exit ramp and drove slowly around the business district until he found a pawnshop on one of the side streets.

Alexa had no idea how much Santini had paid for the rings, but certainly ten times more than the thousand dollars Damas was able to get for them. Alexa could tell from his expression that he wasn't pleased. Apparently the buyer had been aware of the urgency and taken advantage of it.

They hit the first used-car lot at the edge of town and Damas bought a 1974 blue Chevy sedan for six hundred dollars. They switched everything into it and left the rental car in a public parking lot. "I'll let them know later where they can pick it up."

Damas studied the map and then took off again in a zigzag pattern northward, never staying on any stretch of road for more than a couple of hours.

"There's a nice picnic spot," she said as they roared past a tranquil lake surrounded by an expanse of soft green grass.

"No time," he replied with tight lips. They ate on the run as they crossed into Vermont.

The baby turned out to be a good traveler and a source of entertainment. She was bright eyed and playful. She cooed and giggled and was generous with her slobbery openmouthed smiles.

"Good girl," Alexa murmured as Dorrie kicked her chubby little legs and let her change the diaper without protest at their rest stops. Damas smiled his approval as she began to handle the baby with more confidence and pleasure.

"Tell me about your teaching job," he said as he allowed himself a moment's respite from worry.

"Well, I teach history at Hunter College in New York City and spend most of my days in an ugly but charming old building that has gargoyles decorating the entrance doors. I have a small crowded office and a class load that's three times too heavy." She couldn't believe how insignificant her daily irritations seemed now.

He searched her face. "Are you happy you chose to be a teacher?"

"I'm not sure I made the choice," she answered thoughtfully. "My adoptive parents expected it of me. As far as they are concerned education was the right career for me. I never questioned it."

"And now?"

"I don't know." The answer surprised her. A few days ago she would have sworn that her life was exactly as she wanted it to be. Now her well-ordered, self-contained little world had been blown apart. She wasn't the same person anymore. "There are lots of things I'm discovering about myself," she admitted as a blush mounted her cheeks. She brazenly laid a hand on his knee as evidence of her new sexual boldness.

He stiffened at the touch. The remembered softness of her warm curves taunted him. Her honest femininity needed no ploys or guises. Last night her willingness to follow his lead and to give pleasure as readily as to receive it had revealed a startling innocence. There had been no pretenses. Even now as she touched him, he knew that she had little idea what effect she was having upon him. Damn it, he had to keep focused. He pulled away from the contact.

She was surprised and withdrew her hand. With a slight tremble to her chin, she looked straight ahead and folded her hands in her lap. "No matter what happens," she said, "I'm glad about last night."

With an indifference he didn't feel, he shrugged. "You may have misled yourself. People act differently under stress."

He felt her recoil and he damned himself for his bluntness. He should have waited, but knew that once back in her own environment, she might feel differently about him and what had happened between them.

He glanced at her lovely profile and saw the quiver in her inviting lips. The temptation was strong to pull the car over and try to explain, but he jerked his eyes back to the road. He knew that this wasn't the time to worry about the future. Right now, his biggest problem was getting her safely out of Santini's net. If he failed, neither of them might have much of a future to worry about.

AT THE SAME MOMENT that Damas crossed the Vermont state line, Tony Petroni had located their abandoned rental car. A few minutes later, he talked to a salesman who told him that he'd sold a 1974 Chevy sedan to a dark-haired man and blond woman carrying a small baby.

Petroni called Santini.

"WE'D BETTER STOP for gas," Damas said as twilight fell across the wooded landscape. "Wouldn't hurt to load up on food, either." When he saw a convenience store and station just ahead, he turned on his blinkers and glanced in the rearview mirror. Every muscle in his body stiffened. He felt a rigid tightness going across his tired shoulders. Had that dark car been trailing them since the last gas fill-up? The ten-year-old secondhand vehicle they were in couldn't outrun anyone intent on catching up with them.

He passed the gas station, and when he came to the next junction, he took a hard right. The black Seville went right on by. He let out his breath. Better stick to back roads until nightfall.

He turned to Alexa. "Look on the map and find the next town of any size." He glanced at the gas tank. Less than a fourth full.

"There's one about forty-five miles from the junction we just passed."

"Are we going to keep driving all night."

He made a calculated decision. "No, we'll stop, get a few hours' sleep and then do some early-morning driving."

Streetlights were already on when they reached a nice-size Vermont town nestled in a narrow valley. Instead of stopping at a motel on the outskirts, Damas drove to the center of town, where there was lots of traffic noise and blinking neon lights.

The modest Kennedy Hotel was located on a corner and surrounded by small businesses. Damas drove past it, then came back and parked the car around the corner about a half block from the hotel's side entrance. He helped Alexa out of the car and took the baby out of her car seat. They walked back to the hotel and entered by the side door. "I'll bring the things up later."

The place was obviously a resident hotel, with several older people visible in the lobby and halls.

"Yes, there's a room available," the thin gray-haired desk clerk told them.

After Damas signed the register as Mr. and Mrs. Joe Williams, they quickly made their way up to the second floor by way of a slow-moving elevator.

The room they had been given was at the back of the hotel, with two tall windows overlooking an alley. Damas surveyed the alley in both directions, then pulled down the shades. Then he turned on a couple of orangish lights.

"Be back in a minute."

He walked the length of the hall in both directions and checked the stairway for a quick exit. Alexa watched his precautions with rising uneasiness. Like an animal, he prowled, taking the stairs up to the third floor and back down to the first. His face was grim, his concentration total. Finally, satisfied, he went down to the car and brought up some of their provisions.

"We don't have any way to heat water," she reminded him. The boiled water was almost gone.

"There's a small café two doors down," he said. "As soon as it's dark, we'll get something to eat and ask them to boil some water for us." He nodded toward the bed. "Grab a nap. I'll watch the baby."

Alexa didn't argue. This cold, obsessive man was becoming a stranger. Withdrawn, preoccupied, he even handled the baby in a detached manner as he sat down. After he'd taken out his .38 revolver, he laid it on a table beside his chair and faced the door, ready and poised. It was as if he could smell danger in the air.

She stretched out on the bed and at last a bone-deep fatigue drew her into a restless sleep. She must have slept a couple of hours. When she awoke, Damas still sat facing the door, but the baby was asleep on the bed beside her. Damas's dark eyebrows were pulled together in a frown and the creases around his mouth had deepened. She was painfully conscious of the weight that she had placed on his shoulders.

Impulsively she left the bed and knelt at his feet. "Damas, what can I do? Don't shut me out. Please... please let me be close to you."

He pulled her up into his lap and cradled her in his arms. As she laid her head against his shoulder, she couldn't keep the tears back. He stroked her hair and placed a kiss on her forehead, but she sensed that his mind was somewhere else. What he didn't need was a sobbing female on his hands, she lectured herself.

Wiping her eyes, she raised her head from his chest. She resisted the impulse to stroke his rigid cheeks and jutted chin. "What happens now?"

He glanced at his watch. "I guess we have to eat."

"It's the accepted activity for filling empty stomachs. We'll both feel better after some hot food," she said in her practical tone. "A sizzling steak loaded with fat and high cholesterol and mashed potatoes smothered in thick gravy—that's what we need. And I'm buying. I've got forty-five dollars to blow."

A flicker of amusement softened the hard glint in his eyes. "In that case, what are we waiting for?"

The Oriole Café was a mom-and-pop business offering a plain but substantial menu. Damas picked a table at the back of the narrow restaurant and took a chair facing the door. He let his jacket fall free and Alexa knew his .38 was within reach. The knowledge could have cooled her appetite, but there was an air of unreality about the whole situation. Ordinary people in the small café were laughing and chatting. The bustling, spry little waitress was more than happy to wash bottles and boil water for the baby. Dorrie sat in a infant chair hooked to the end of the table and Damas gave her a spoon. She slobbered on it happily while they ate.

Damas never completely relaxed, but the lines in his taut cheeks eased, even as he kept an eye on the door. Alexa tried her best to keep the conversation centered on food and restaurants. When he made a few casual remarks about his favorite spot near Times Square, she said, "You'll have to take me there sometime. After all, you'll owe me a dinner."

He reached across the table and squeezed her hand. "Thanks."

"For what?"

"For being you."

She gazed at her plate so he wouldn't see the tears flooding her eyes. He didn't argue when she took the check. Holding the baby, he waited at the cash register while she paid the bill and then cautiously looked up and down the street as they exited the café.

They had almost gotten to the front door of the hotel, when he suddenly grabbed her arm. "Hurry."

"What is it?"

He didn't answer as he rushed her into the lobby.

"What is it?" she repeated, her heart suddenly pounding like a jackhammer.

"A black Seville...parked halfway down the block." A coincidence? His gut instinct said no. Ready defenses shot into place like a Patriot missile. Instead of stopping at the elevator, he led Alexa past it and out the side door to the spot where they had parked the Chevy.

He opened the passenger door for her, and once she was inside, he thrust the baby into her arms. Then he raced around to the driver's side and gunned the car away from the curb.

"We only brought the diaper bag," she protested, glancing back at the hotel. She'd washed out Mia's pink jumpsuit and hung it in the shower stall. The supply of formula, bottle liners, packages of disposable diapers and leftover snacks had been left behind.

Damas's thoughts raced like leaves whipped in a gale wind. Was he overreacting? There must be dozens of black cars in every town. Why did he think that the one they'd passed on the highway had found them? How could anyone possibly know they were within a hundred miles of this place? But somebody did. He was positive of it.

"They've gotten a make on this car. We'll have to ditch it."

He drove through the labyrinth of streets as if he knew where he was going in the strange town. She was mystified until she remembered how he had pored over the telephone book in the hotel room. At the time she had thought he was searching for someone's number, but he must have been studying a local map and memorizing some locations. He brought the car to an abrupt stop at the bus station.

"Stay here," he ordered as he bounded out of the car and disappeared inside. A moment later he was back with two tickets in his hands. "Come on."

He took the baby and the diaper bag and pulled Alexa quickly around the side of the building to where travelers were lined up to get on a bus. They boarded, too, and he installed her and the baby in a rear seat near the emergency doors. He remained standing in the aisle until all the passengers were seated and the driver had shut the door. Then he sat down beside her, turning his head around so he could look out the back window, his eyes fixed on the bus station.

Dorrie had patiently endured all the jostling, but as the bus lurched forward, she decided that enough was enough. She managed a few lusty yells that had nearby passengers shaking their heads in exasperation. *Not a squalling baby all night.*

Alexa fished out one of the bottles that had been made up in the restaurant. Dorrie quickly settled down when the bottle was popped in her mouth. She lay in Alexa's arms and greedily sucked the formula.

Damas laid his head back against the seat and closed his eyes. Alexa knew he was as far from falling asleep as anyone could be. "Where are we going?"

"About fifty miles down the road," he answered without looking at her.

"What's there?"

"Probably nothing...but that's where we're getting off the bus."

Chapter Sixteen

The lights of the bus faded in the distance, leaving Damas and Alexa in shadows as they stood by the side of the road. The area seemed to be a rural one, with pinpoints of light identifying houses spread far apart, and open land in between.

What are we doing here? she wanted to scream at him. As long as they'd been on the bus, they'd been moving closer and closer to Bar Harbor. Now they were on foot, in the middle of nowhere. She'd lost all track of time. Even with the nap she'd had at the hotel, she was dead tired. She shivered in the night air. The landscape around them was unreal. A tiny eyelash of a moon was lost in swift clouds moving across the sky. Tall trees swayed in the wind, making a rumbling sound like that of a distant ocean.

She was bewildered, and furious with Damas for not sharing his thoughts with her. Rigid and uncommunicative, he had sat beside her on the bus like some stranger. All her efforts to get him to talk to her had failed. Most of the time he didn't even seem aware that she was there.

"What now?" she demanded ungraciously as she watched him scan the land around them.

He shifted the sleeping baby on his shoulder and pointed to a small cluster of lights in the distance. "We'll head that way. Looks like we'll find a town there. Can't be more than a couple of miles. Come on."

He started out at a brisk pace and she had trouble keeping up with his long stride. Her agitation grew with every weary step. Finally she grabbed his arm and pulled him to a stop.

"Talk to me! Tell me what we're doing out here in the middle of no place. I'm not taking another step until you do."

Moonlight flickered across his face, adding shadows to the already deep creases around his mouth. At first she thought he was going to challenge her threat, but he slowly let out his breath and surprised her by saying, "I'm sorry...I didn't mean to keep you in the dark. I just didn't want to worry you."

She laughed outright. "Heaven forbid. I love being on foot with only borrowed clothes on my back. I shouldn't be the least worried that we're stranded in the middle of the night."

He took her arm. "Come on. I'll fill you in while we walk. I don't know how in the hell Santini's men got a fix on us, but they did. We must have been just a bit ahead of them all day. They must have found the rental car we ditched and located the lot where we bought the Chevy. If I hadn't noticed the license plate as the black Seville went by us at the junction I wouldn't have recognized the automobile as the same one parked just beyond the hotel when we came back from the restaurant.''

"You mean they were sitting there waiting for us?''

"More likely they had arranged a welcoming committee in our room. I'm sure we would have walked into a reception if we'd blissfully gone upstairs. We bought ourselves a little time by going out the side door, but not much.''

"But how will they know we took the bus?''

"They'll find the car, and if they flash a picture of me around, the ticket guy will remember he sold me two tickets to Denville. Once the bus arrives there about eight o'clock in the morning, they'll meet it—but we won't be on it. The driver will tell them that we got off, but he'll probably be vague about the exact spot, because there were no identifying markers where he let us out. They'll double back and try to pick up our trail again.''

"And they'll find us here in the middle of nowhere.'' She took a couple of deep breaths to steady her voice. He might quit talking to her if she gave in to a rising panic.

"We've bought ourselves a little time. Not much . . . but maybe enough.'' He put his arm around her shoulders and held her against his side as they walked. "We can't go this alone anymore. We would have had a chance if Santini didn't know where to look . . . but he does. He'll be able to pinpoint our location. I know Leo. He'll put in place a net that even a mosquito couldn't get through.''

"What are we going to do?''

"There's nothing we can do but ask for help.''

"I thought you said your superior wouldn't get involved. Is there a chance he'll change his mind?"

"Not in a million years. Talbot has already made his stand," Damas said grimly. "He'll never forgive me for sacrificing nearly two years' work to get the goods on Santini. And we almost had him. A few more documents and we could have pinned his hide to the courtroom wall. No, we can't look to Captain Talbot. He knows that this alleged kidnapping is a loaded bomb ready to explode. If I try to go over his head I'll get the same answer."

"Then who?"

"I'm going to gamble on an old friend who went through police academy with me, Sheriff Jack Powers. Jack didn't like being a city cop and went back home to Vermont. A couple of years ago he sent me a Christmas card telling me he had been elected sheriff of a small county in Vermont. And that's where we are now. I've decided we have no choice but to give old Jack a call, tell him what's up and persuade him to send a car after us. With an escort, we can make it to Bar Harbor in spite of Santini."

"Do you think he'll do it?"

"I wouldn't call him if I didn't think so," he answered flatly.

Relief brought new energy coursing through her. The nightmare would soon be over. As they walked down the country road, her mind sped ahead. After they put the baby into Mia's arms, what then? Damas had said everything would be different when life returned to normal. He had already warned her that she shouldn't trust her feelings under the circumstances. Maybe danger had changed her, made her more vulnerable. She looked up into his face, felt the warmth of his body as he strode beside her, and her chest tightened with emotion. She loved him. No matter what happened after their mission was over, she knew her feelings for him wouldn't change.

They passed a small lake reflecting moonlight on its rippling surface. Several boats were tethered along its banks and a deserted boat house rose darkly against the waters. A smattering of houses, buildings and stores extended away from the lake along haphazard streets. All dark.

It was true, thought Alexa. Some places really did roll up the sidewalks at night. After the never-ending bustle of New York City, the hushed silence was eerie. Their footsteps sounded loudly on the cement sidewalks and several dogs responded with a cacophony of barking.

They kept walking until the neon lights of a small bar flashed out into the deserted sidewalk and street. Two cars and an old pickup truck were parked out in front. This oasis of light was the only sign of habitation in the small village.

Damas pointed to a bench leaning against an old building next to the bar, which was undoubtedly used during the day by idle people watchers. "I think it would be better if you waited outside while I telephone Jack." He handed her the sleeping baby. "A single fellow won't cause much interest. As soon as I contact him, we'll find a place to wait until he can come pick us up."

She nodded.

"It's going to be all right," he assured her as she sat down on the bench. He kissed her lightly on the forehead. "Don't go anywhere."

She gave him a wry smile. "I wouldn't think of it."

There were only two men in the bar, the bartender and an old codger who wore a beat-up straw hat and had his long legs wrapped around a bar stool. They were talking sports in a spirited dispute. The long-legged fellow motioned for Damas to sit down and join in.

"You look like an intelligent fellow," he said. "Tell this misguided Washington Redskins lover that his team hasn't got a snowball's chance in hell of getting to the Super Bowl this year."

Damas forced himself to participate in the banter for a couple of minutes. Then he said casually, "I need to use your phone."

The bartender nodded toward a rotary phone sitting on the edge of the bar. "You can use that one."

Nicely placed so eavesdropping was unavoidable.

"Better not," Damas said with a smile. "Long-distance call. I'd better shove some coins in a pay phone."

The bartender shrugged. "Guess you could hike down to the lake. There's a public one by the boat house."

Damas kept a smile on his face. "Thanks. Nice talking with you."

As Damas went out the door, they began arguing about a truck somebody had for sale.

Alexa greeted him with a hopeful expression. "Did you . . . ? Is Jack . . . ?"

"No to both questions. I couldn't make the call. Two guys had their ears cocked for every word. We'll have to walk back to the lake. The bartender said there's a pay phone there."

He took the baby and they retraced their steps to the lake. Water lapping and sucking against the shore made an eerie sound like a silent beast waiting for its prey. The skin on Alexa's neck prickled and she stayed close to Damas's side. They saw the telephone booth in the dim light of a single bulb above the locked door of the boat house.

Damas transferred the baby again to Alexa and she leaned against the outside wall. He fished in his pocket for money, lifted the receiver and then swore vehemently.

"What's the matter?"

"The blasted thing is out of order."

Alexa closed her eyes. Her arms ached, her back was arched in a painful stance and the weight of Dorrie was almost unbearable. She wanted to sink to the ground and bury her head in her hands.

"We'll have to go back," Damas said in a tight, exasperated tone. "I'll have to use the phone in the bar. There's no other choice unless we wait for morning. Not a good idea, because that would delay Jack's getting to us. The bartender probably spreads news faster than Western Union, but we'll have to chance alerting the town to our whereabouts."

They walked back to the bar. The same neon lights flashed in the windows, but the place was locked up tight. The two cars were gone and only the old truck with a For Sale in the window remained in front of the building.

Alexa slumped down on the bench with the baby. Damas pounded on the front door of the bar as though threatening to bash it in if it didn't open. The noise echoed down the street, but nobody came.

He swung around, his shoulders tense and his hands clenched at his side. He stared at the dilapidated pickup. With a couple of long strides, he reached the driver's side and jerked open the door. He put his head down under the dash, and after several frustrating tries, he managed to hot-wire the ignition. As the old engine rumbled and snorted, he yelled at Alexa to get in.

Surely someone would hear the noise and take after them, worried Alexa as she climbed in with the baby, but the streets remained as empty as ever. Damas headed the pickup back toward the highway. She was so relieved to be off her feet that she didn't care how much the rickety old truck shook every bone in her body.

Damas had little faith that the old vehicle would take them very far. The gas gauge was on empty, but it was a good guess that it wasn't even working. When they reached the highway, he urged the truck at a vibrating speed of forty miles an hour for about ten miles until the lights of a truck stop loomed ahead.

So far, so good, he thought. If the old pickup didn't conk out in the next half mile, he'd be on the phone to Jack within a few minutes.

Chapter Seventeen

Damas's mind raced as he turned off the highway. The truck stop had been built where two paved highways made a junction. Several semitrailers were parked like huge box cars in front of a combination café and gas station. Damas drove slowly past the parked rigs to an economy motel sitting on an adjoining lot behind the truck stop.

Without saying anything to Alexa, he got out of the pickup, walked hurriedly to the unit marked Office and went in. At Damas's request, a sleepy desk clerk assigned him to room twenty-four, first floor, at the back of the building. He got back in the pickup and Alexa looked at him in surprise.

"Is it safe to stop here?"

"We have to wait somewhere for Jack." He'd gambled that it would be less risky to stop in the middle of nowhere to call his friend, but that little scheme had gone up like a puff of smoke. He couldn't afford to repeat the fiasco of the past few hours. At least they'd gotten some different transportation, and the old pickup truck standing out in front of their motel room was a good decoy. All they needed was a little safe time, a place to hole up in until Jack could send an escort for them. He knew that the chances were great that Santini's men would be checking every motel on that route.

Alexa quickly settled Dorrie in another makeshift chair bed while Damas tried to use the telephone.

"Damn," he swore. The switchboard was closed for the night. "I'll have to call Jack from the café. I saw a couple of phone booths out in front."

Instant panic fled into her face and her tired lower lip quivered as if she were fighting back a plea for him not to leave her.

He took her in his arms and held her tightly. "You'll be all right here."

"But what about you? What if someone is on the lookout for you?"

"I'll have to chance it. Once I get the call through to Jack, help will be on the way." Then he said gruffly, "If I shouldn't come back—"

"Don't talk like that!"

"Listen to me. You'll be safe if you stay out of sight. If something should go wrong, stay here until the sheriff's men come for you. You can trust Jack Powers to take you and the baby safely to Bar Harbor." He buried his face in her soft neck and then raised his mouth to hers. His kiss was brief but intense. His voice was husky as he pulled away. "I've got to make that call now."

He stopped at the door and looked back at her. Her eyes were large and misty, her slender body a lovely balance of curves and planes. "Be back in a few minutes," he said.

SHERIFF POWERS did *not* like being aroused in the middle of the night, Damas was told in no uncertain terms when he reached the county sheriff's switchboard. Any message would be delivered to him first thing in the morning. Damas's refusal to leave a message only resulted in an impatient dismissal by the tired woman on the other end of the line. "Sorry, sir... try again in the morning."

Damas hung up, leaning his head against the cool metal of the telephone box. Damn... After a moment he straightened up. Maybe there was a chance that his home phone was listed. Nothing under Jack Powers, he discovered when he called Information. What was Jack's wife's name? Alice? Arlene? Maybe their home phone was listed under her name? He called Information again. The hunch paid off. He was given a number for Arlene Powers.

Jack's sleep-gruff voice barked "Hello" after the second ring.

Damas gave a relieved laugh. "Wake up, old buddy."

"Who in the hell is this?"

"Your old designated driver. Remember the guy always on hand to drive you home when you got stinking drunk on screwdrivers?"

"Silva! You old son of a gun. What the hell you doing waking me up in the middle of the night to shoot the breeze?"

"It's business, Jack. Bad business."

His voice changed and he became alert and serious. "What's up?"

Damas told him as succinctly as he could why he was on the run with a woman pretending to be Leo Santini's wife.

Jack gave a low whistle. "I can see why the department doesn't want to touch it with a ten-foot pole. I can't quite believe you'd go out on a limb like that. Doesn't sound like the guy I knew who could love 'em and leave 'em."

"This is different."

"It must be. What do you want me to do?"

Damas explained his desperate need for an escort. "Santini's men are all over the place. I've got to get the baby to her mother in Bar Harbor, Maine, as quickly as possible. My superior has agreed to put Mia and the child into protective custody so Leo can't get at them. I thought I could make it without help, but somehow Santini's guys spotted us yesterday and we've been on the run all night."

"Where are you now?"

Damas told him.

Jack gave another low whistle. "You're out of my jurisdiction, buddy. No way I can waltz into that county with my men. The sheriff there is an old codger who has territorial obsessions. He'd raise a stink as high as the state capitol."

"I thought we were in your county. That's why we got off the bus when we did."

"Nope . . . you're about thirty miles short."

"Damn it, I shouldn't have trusted my memory. Everything happened so fast. We were on the bus before I had a chance to look at a map."

"I tell you what. You hightail it down the road to Blairville. That's just across the county line. I'll do some calling and have somebody meet you there in about an hour.''

A heavy weight slipped off Damas's back. Victory was almost within their grasp. "You got it!''

He hung up the receiver and hurriedly left the phone booth. His keen intuitive sense was dulled by optimism, and as he passed one of the parked rigs, too late he glimpsed a raised arm that came out of the shadows.

He tried to spin away. Out of the corner of his eye he saw the black wrench coming down. He threw up an arm, but not soon enough. The blow hit him solid on the side of the head.

His knees buckled.

Someone gave a hoarse laugh of satisfaction.

Fireworks exploded behind his eyes. Pain shot like rockets from one side of his skull to the other. Parts of his body floated away as a rolling mist deepened into blackness.

Chapter Eighteen

Alexa lay down on the bed without taking off her clothes. She was physically and emotionally exhausted. Her mind replayed over and over again fragmented pieces of their flight. One scene blended into the other like watery images, overlapping and blurred. With great effort, she tried to focus on her immediate perceptions as a way of anchoring herself to the moment. She listened to the swish of cars going by on the highway, the sound of a door closing and footsteps on the second-floor balcony and the rumbling of a heavy truck pulling out onto the highway. The sound of the baby's relaxed deep breathing, the comfortable support of the bed and the anticipation of Damas's returning footsteps combined to ease the tension in her weary body. The ordeal was almost over. Once the sheriff's escort arrived, they would be whisked to Bar Harbor without delay. She would put Dorrie into Mia's arms and the two of them would be safe from Leo's tyranny. Whatever the future held, the three of them would face it together as a family.

She closed her eyes. And there would be Damas in her life. Even though he had warned her that things would look differently when they were out of danger, he had awakened her as a woman capable of love and passion. She would fight to keep him in her life. He would be back in a few minutes.

She drew a long deep breath and a quiver of expectation went through her. He would take her in his arms, tenderly undress her as he had done before, and they would find the pleasure that the miracle of love had given to them. Lost in the fantasy of remembered happiness, she began to relax and wasn't even aware when sleep overtook her.

When she awakened the baby was whimpering and bright sunlight edged the drawn draperies. She sat straight up. It was morning. She must have been asleep for hours. Shock like a cold blast of ice water hit her.

Damas!

She jerked to her feet and ran across the room to the bathroom. Empty. She covered her mouth to keep from screaming his name. Where was he?

Dorrie's cries rose in angry protest as she demanded attention. Alexa picked the baby up, her thoughts spinning out in every direction. What had happened? Had she been too deeply asleep to know when he came back? Maybe Damas had returned as promised and then left again to bring back some breakfast.

Her eyes darted to the bed. A single imprint where she had been lying. Her lip trembled. Even in her deepest sleep, she would have known if he had gathered her into his arms.

He had not come back! The truth shot through her head like a sharp pain. Something had happened. Dear God, where was he? Her first impulse was to go rushing out the door. She had to find him. The echo of his command stopped her in the middle of the floor.

If something should go wrong, stay here!

She bit her lip hard enough to taste a trickle of blood. Every instinct told her she should pick up the baby and run. Why had he made her promise to stay and wait for help if he didn't come back?

She paced with the crying baby. "Yes, yes, don't cry...don't cry...everything is just fine." Her tearful babbling did little to soothe the hungry baby. On some detached level her insides felt as if she were being battered in a dozen directions at once.

Get ahold of yourself. Take care of the baby. Her movements were automatic as she changed Dorrie's diaper and took the last bottle out of the diaper bag. While Dorrie gulped her breakfast, Alexa stared unseeing at the floor as terrifying scenarios went through her mind. A hundred different things could have happened. She knew that Damas had planned to be back in a few minutes. He had told her that the sheriff would send someone to escort them. Had he made the call to Jack Powers? Was anybody coming?

The minutes trickled by with agonizing slowness. When there was a brisk knock on the door. She let out a grateful sob. Sheriff Powers and his men had arrived.

Holding the baby in her arms, she opened the door and nearly fainted.

"Good morning, Mrs. Santini." A smirking Malchek, nodding, holding his chauffeur's cap in his hand. Behind him, two men leaned against a black Seville, watching.

She stared at them in disbelief and tightened her hold on the baby. "No—"

"We're here to take you to your husband."

DAMAS CAME BACK to consciousness with the smell of farm produce in his nostrils. A complete absence of light made it impossible to tell where he was. The hard surface on which he lay was not the ground—he knew that. He opened and shut his eyes several times, as if the repeated effort would bring his vision into focus. Nothing changed. He moved his arms out in a sweeping motion and touched a flat surface. He ran his fingers over the rough exterior. Cardboard, he thought. A box. His hand touched another one. A stack of boxes. The strong green smell told him what they contained. He must be in a storeroom of some kind. A windowless storeroom, filled with boxes of fresh produce.

This deduction made him feel less vulnerable. At least he was alive and able to think. He raised his hand and gingerly touched the open wound on his head. Blood had clotted in his hair and had coated the cheek on which he had been lying. Very carefully, he sat up.

Pain ricocheted like a tennis ball inside his skull. He pulled up his legs and leaned his head against his knees. Nausea churned his stomach. He feared he was close to passing out again. Waves of weakness came and went for a long time before he was able to feel his body becoming whole once more. His thoughts cleared. He forced himself to remember.

The call to Jack had not gone as planned. His friend could not help them until they crossed the county line into his jurisdiction. That's what Damas had planned to do. Load up Alexa and the baby in the truck. Get on the road again and drive as fast as the old pickup would take them to the small town where Jack and his men would meet them.

He held his aching head in his hands. He cursed himself for being such a fool. He'd forgotten to be careful. The blow had come out of nowhere. He had walked too close to the parked truck. The raised hand and black wrench came back all too sharply. While he was telephoning Jack, someone had spied on him.

He groaned as the result of his carelessness became clear. Alexa and the baby! The motel was small enough that someone could knock on every door until they found them. She wouldn't leave. She would do as he had ordered. Why had he told her to stay there? *Because you thought Jack's men would come for her.*

He willed himself to his feet. Taking a few stumbling steps, he lurched against the stack of boxes and held on to them for balance. There had to be a door into the storage room. Feeling his way in the total darkness, he made it past the stacked boxes to a smooth wall. With his hands pressed against it, he eased along, cautiously moving his feet sideways as he felt his way.

He was completely unprepared for the loud rumbling noise and the jolt that threw him to the floor. As he lay there with his bloody cheek pressed against the vibrating floor, he knew that he wasn't in a storage room. Someone had tossed him into a semitrailer loaded with boxes of farm produce.

THE VERMONT LANDSCAPE swept by as Alexa sat in the back seat of the Seville with a man on each side of her. Before entering the car she had demanded, "Where's Damas?"

Malchek had snorted. "Really stupid, letting himself be seen by a trucker. The boss has more friends in the Teamsters' union than bees in a hive. Once the word and his picture went out, every driver between there and New York was on the lookout for him. And one of them hit pay dirt." Malchek gave an ugly laugh. "Now your new lover boy is going on a little trip. C.O.D. You go through bodyguards pretty fast. Keeps us busy."

They were going to kill Damas. Arrange an accident, the way they had with Guy.

Malchek grinned as all warmth drained from her face. Pain curled in the middle of her chest. She wanted to scream and scrape her finger across the ugly man's face. "What have you done with him?"

"You can ask your husband all about it," Malchek sneered. "He's waiting for you at the farm."

Farm? Her mind refused to function. As the miles rolled by, she felt nothing but utter despair. Because the heartache was so intense, her thoughts became strangely detached, as if her mind had shut down.

From the curt exchanges between the men, she knew that their destination wasn't very far away. Apparently Santini had a Vermont farm as one of his secluded residences. Very soon she was going to meet him face-to-face. She should be frightened, she told her numbed inner self. He was a cruel, harsh man who would deal with her the way he dealt with other people who tried to cross him.

A flicker of satisfaction accompanied the thought that at least Mia would be safe. If her sister had been taken into protective custody, Santini wouldn't be able to vent his rage on her. When he discovered he had the wrong woman, his wrath would fall on Alexa alone. Once she had been terrified that such a thing might happen. Now she didn't care. She welcomed the opportunity to tell him to his face what she thought of him and the way he had treated Mia. He wouldn't get away with killing Damas . . . unless he killed her, too.

She looked down at the baby and tears sprang to her eyes. She had been willing to endure anything to get Dorrie away from Leo's murderous clutches, but now it was too late. She had tried and failed. And Damas was paying the price for that failure.

DAMAS SAT with his head in his hands, trying to keep the pain from rolling from side to side like a bowling ball. The roar of the engine and whining tires entered his ears like an attacking force. There was no way to get away from it. No way to clear his mind and ears of the unrelenting noise and vibration. He kept reminding himself that the truck would stop eventually. He could only guess when and where he would be disposed of in true Santini fashion. His boss liked things done simply—he knew that. No bullet-ridden bodies or other foul means that translated into obvious murder. The mobster preferred hit-and-runs, drownings and carefully arranged suicides. Santini kept his nose clean. That was the problem. All the months of undercover had not brought to light the records that the FBI needed to nail him. Damas knew he had been getting close. He had eliminated many of Santini's activities as pure subterfuges, and with a little more digging, he might have had proof of Santini's illegal activities. If he had not decided to help Alexa get the baby to her mother, if he had not fallen in love, if he—

He pressed his fingertips against his temples to shut out the nettlesome speculation. He'd made the choices that his conscience had dictated. If he had been able to save them from Leo's clutches, all would have been worth it. But he knew as well as he knew his own fate that he had failed.

THE BLACK SEVILLE turned off the main highway and headed down a road that bit deeply into the country-side. Wooded hills cupped a narrow valley, lush and green with June wildflowers, tall grasses and rolling farmland. The car followed a narrow stream until the valley narrowed and thick stands of spruce, firs and hemlock crowded the road like dark sentinels. The car slowed down at a guarded gate and then followed a curved road to a two-story large redbrick house. Numerous outbuildings that included a barn, stable and a large garage were scattered behind the main house. Wide wooden steps led to a wide white porch that hugged the front of the lovely old farmhouse. Potted geraniums were splashes of red color along the walk. Green fields stretched away from the house in a bu-colic scene that would have been appropriate on a Vermont postcard.

"The boss ain't here yet," Malchek muttered. The disappointment in his voice made it clear he'd hoped for a stormy scene the minute he delivered Mrs. Santini to her husband.

The two men got out and held a door open for Alexa. She had just eased out of the car with the baby, when the front door opened and a furious Clara marched down the steps. Her face was red and blotchy from anger and her fat lips quivered as if she wanted to spit venom in Alexa's face. No doubt she'd been feeling the heat for having let the baby get away.

With stubborn foolishness, Alexa brushed by the woman without relinquishing her hold on the baby. She mounted the steps as if she had every right to carry Dorrie into the house.

Clara stomped into the house behind her.

Once inside the wide front hall, Alexa stopped, not having the vaguest idea where to go and what to do. Fortunately a small older woman dressed in gray and wearing a white apron came through one of the doorways with an anxious look on her wizened face.

"Mr. Santini said you're to have the corner bedroom," she announced quickly. "It's all made up, ma'am. I hope your stay will be a pleasant one." Every line in her narrow face was at odds with the optimistic welcome.

The woman didn't act as if she knew Mia, thought Alexa, so maybe her sister had never been there. Dorrie took that moment to throw one of her tantrums. Alexa knew the baby was wet and needed a bath. Trying to cope with her was more than she could manage. Reluctantly she turned and handed her to Clara.

A gleam of satisfaction crossed the nanny's face as she hugged the baby to her fat chest. Her curt nod said loudly that from now on she'd make sure that the baby wasn't out of her presence.

"If you'd like to freshen up, Mrs. Santini." The gray-haired woman's gaze registered Alexa's cheap jeans and boy's shirt. "I'm Alma. If you'll come this way."

Alexa followed the slight woman up the wide stairs to a large bedroom in the front corner of the house. Tastefully done in homespun Early-American decor, the room was exactly right for the large farmhouse. Under other circumstances Alexa would have appreciated the old-fashioned mahogany furniture, which included a lovely high-backed rocking chair. There was an adjoining modern bathroom, with brass towel racks and a marble basin. She was surprised to see Mia's luggage from the hotel stacked in a large walk-in closet.

"I didn't know whether I should unpack your things or not, Mrs. Santini," Alma said anxiously.

Alexa sat down listlessly on the edge of the bed. "No, that's fine." As soon as Leo got there, there wouldn't be any need for any more pretense. She would greet him as Alexa Widmire. He would take one look at her and know that she was telling the truth— she was not his wife.

Alexa watched from the upstairs window when Santini arrived about an hour later. His large iron gray head emerged from the limousine, followed by his thick trunk and stocky legs. A cold shiver like a snake wound around Alexa's chest. For a moment she could hardly breathe. Her stomach lurched as if she were about to throw up. The danger she was in had never really hit her until that moment.

She backed away from the window, afraid he would look up and see her.

Very deliberately she washed her face, pulled her hair back in a twist and fastened it. She smoothed the collar of her shirt and stood straight in her boy's jeans. Then she turned and walked out of the room and down the stairs. Several doors opened onto the wide front hall and she heard men's voices somewhere in the depths of the house. She followed them and was surprised when they led her to a half-opened door and a set of narrow stairs descending into a basement. The voices faded to a murmur.

She stood there for a long moment and then quietly and purposefully went down the stairs. The basement was an old one. If a cupboard had not been pulled away from the wall, revealing a door and a brightly lit modern room, she would have thought that there was nothing of interest in the old basement.

She carefully moved forward, staying close to the wall, out of the splash of light coming from the inner room. She could hear the men in heated exchange about the best place to keep books and records.

"Nobody's going to look for them here. I've got them under lock and key. The feds can't search the premises without probable cause. No judge is going to give them a warrant to go on a fishing expedition."

The two men went on talking, and even though the conversation made little sense to Alexa, one thing came through loud and clear. The records Damas had been seeking were only a few feet from her.

She turned and stealthily made her way up the stairs, back to her bedroom. When Leo found out he had been duped and his child nearly kidnapped, he would deal with her in short order. No one crossed Santini without paying for it. Damas had put his own life on the line because of her. Thinking about his courage confirmed a decision that was forming in her sharp mind.

She stared out the bedroom window. Her arms were rigid at her sides, her fists clenched. What kind of stupidity had lulled her into an acceptance of the situation? Why was she cowering in her room, waiting until Santini chose to confront her? What did she have to lose if she carried the impersonation further?

She moved away from the window and walked to the closet. Her mouth was set in a determined line as she took out one of Mia's suitcases and placed it on the bed. She was suddenly calm and strangely at peace. It was too soon for the impersonation to be over. She straightened her shoulders. Leo Santini's wife had some unfinished business to take care of.

Chapter Nineteen

Budge Malone whistled "Happy Days Are Here Again" as he drove his rig ten miles over the speed limit. About midafternoon someone plastered a flyer on his windshield when he had stopped to fill his rig with gas. Lo and behold, when he'd pulled up at the Junction for a mug of java at three o'clock in the morning, there was the guy pictured in the flyer, heading to the phone booth. He had let out a low whistle, got himself a wrench and waited. A few minutes later he rang the number listed on the flyer.

"I've got the merchandise you wanted."

There was a grunt of satisfaction on the other end and he'd been given the address of a warehouse about a half a day's drive. He glanced at the dashboard clock. One more hour to collection time.

Budge was familiar with this stretch of highway and knew about the railroad crossing, so he slowed down when he saw a school bus stopped in front of the tracks. A second later he was puzzled. No sign of a train coming, no flashing lights. He couldn't see why the bus was just sitting there. He swore as he brought his rig to a sudden stop behind the bus.

DAMAS WAS thrown forward as the rig's brakes grabbed and the semitrailer stopped abruptly. Instantly every sense was alert. He staggered to his feet. In numerous explorations of the half-filled truck, he had located the back doors. That's the way they had put him in, he reasoned, and that's the way they would take him out. Had the truck reached its destination? Like a caged animal waiting for the keeper to unlock a cage, he waited, ready to spring.

WHEN THE BUS didn't move, Malone glanced in his rearview mirror. He shifted gears, ready to go around the stalled vehicle. He saw two cars were coming up quickly behind him. One vehicle swung out into the other lane and stopped beside him; the other pinned him from behind. Too late, he realized it was a setup. Someone was going to take his expensive merchandise away from him.

Cursing, he reached for the revolver in his glove compartment. Just as he drew the gun out, both doors to his cab opened and steel hands clamped down on his arms.

Damas heard the engine die. A moment later muffled voices came from outside the rear of the truck. A scrape of metal sounded on the large doors. *They were going to open them.* He stood waiting. His strangled breath came in short gulps. He winced against the throbbing pain in his head.

The doors swung open. An onslaught of lights blinded him. He hurled himself like a tackler at the figure who stood just outside the truck. The force of his weight threw both of them to the ground and they rolled on the hard pavement. Damas fought like a wild animal and was gaining the upper edge, when two other men pinned him to the ground and freed the man he'd tackled.

Sheriff Jack Powers rose to his feet, massaging his chin where Damas had landed a hard jab. "Hold on, Silva! Is this the thanks I get for saving your doggone hide?"

DAMAS SAT in the sheriff's office and winced as Dr. Vought tended to the open wound on his skull. "Can't tell about a concussion without X rays," the doctor said, putting on a bandage where he had shaved away a large hank of Damas's thick hair.

"I'm fine," Damas said through gritted teeth. He knew he was damn lucky. Jack had told him that after Damas had hung up, Jack had phoned a friend who lived near the Junction truck stop and asked him to go over to the motel. Malone's truck had already left by the time Jack's man got there, but in the bright light coming through the café windows, a pool of wet blood was visible on the pavement. Another driver had seen Malone's rig pull out from that spot just as he had pulled in.

A helicopter located Malone's semi on the highway and Sheriff Powers quickly set up the trap to intercept it. Damas was grateful for the rescue, but worry over Alexa and the baby made the victory a small one. Several witnesses had seen a woman and infant getting into a large black car at the motel with three men.

"They've taken her to Santini. All hell will break loose when he finds out he's got the wrong woman. We've got to get to her first. Have you put out an APB on the black Seville?'' Damas demanded with a clenched jaw.

"Take it easy, buddy. I still remember a few things from the academy and my time with New York's finest. Besides, we've got an idea where they might have taken her."

Damas was on his feet. "What are we waiting for?"

"Confirmation. We've had reconnaissance in place for several months monitoring Mr. Santini's activities. If a black Seville passes by that point, we'll know it."

A moment later when the telephone rang, Damas almost grabbed it out of Jack's hand. It seemed like an eternity before he nodded and slammed down the receiver.

ALEXA CAME DOWN the center stairs and walked purposefully through an archway, into the spacious living room. An oak-beam ceiling, knotty-pine paneled walls and lovely antique furniture gave the room a friendly, comfortable air, as if any moment a large family of rosy-faced children and smiling parents would gather in front of the fireplace.

Leo had his broad back to her as he poured himself a drink from an old-fashioned serving cart. At the sound of her high heels on the polished oak floor, he turned around. In a deliberate cold appraisal, his eyes traveled from the soft blond hair framing her face, past the low-cut neckline of the expensive blue sheath, down its short length skirt. She saw the heat of lust flash into his icy blue eyes. Instead of being afraid, she felt strangely empowered. She had found his Achilles' heel. Mia. She knew then that his brutal treatment of his wife didn't arise out of indifference to her... and that meant he was vulnerable. Alexa took courage and smiled inwardly. She intended to use that vulnerability. Nothing was important now except the records that would provide the evidence Damas had been seeking.

Santini walked across the room and stopped in front of her. Alexa knew it was the moment of truth. If he detected the slightest difference, he would know the woman standing before him was not his wife. Leo's lustful expression did not change when he slapped her so hard that she was thrown off balance to her knees.

"Slut."

She huddled on the floor in front of him. Her ears rang from the blow. She closed her eyes for a moment to hide flaming anger. She wanted to lurch to her feet and scrape her fingernails across his hard cheek. She might look like Mia, but her reaction to his abuse was not submission. She took deep breaths to clear her head. *Don't blow it.*

When he took hold of her shoulders and pulled her up, she automatically stiffened. Could she keep up the pretense if he continued to abuse her? *You have to! You have to take whatever he gives.*

His thick hands tightened on her shoulders. He shoved his face so close to hers she could smell his nicotine breath.

"Who is Alexa Widmire?"

The question was so unexpected that she froze. Nothing he could have said would have stunned her more.

"Who is she?" He dug his fingers into her shoulders.

Damas had been certain that Leo would send somebody around to her apartment. Once they went through her things, they would find bills in her desk, discover her files and teaching contracts and, more revealing than anything, some photo albums that would show the two identical sisters.

"Answer me!" He raised a threatening hand.

"Don't... don't you know?" she stammered.

"If I knew I wouldn't be wasting my time asking. Why did you call that number from the hotel? My men will be checking it out, but you can tell me yourself... right now!"

She swallowed hard. There was still a little time left... until Leo's men called him. Then it would all be over. "She's... she's a girlfriend," Alexa said evenly. "I... I met her at the beauty shop. We were supposed to get together and I just called her to have someone to talk to."

When he just stared at her, Alexa knew she had been too glib. Mia would have burst into tears and sobbed over his displeasure. His anger would have turned her sister into a whimpering coward. She would have never flung such an explanation at him.

"Cut out the playacting, Mia. You never were any good at it"

Mia! He called her, "Mia." Relief made her knees weak. Because she didn't know what else to do, she pulled away and sat down abruptly on the sofa. She put a hand against the cheek still burning from his blow.

He looked at her thoughtfully, downed his drink and then poured himself another one. "What have your lovers been telling you?"

"I . . . I don't know what you mean."

"Of course you do. I can just hear them. 'Don't let him push you around.' 'Stand up to him.' 'Use the brains in your pretty little head, Mia.'" He bent his glowering face over her. "Only we know you don't have any brains, don't we?" He forced her chin up with his hand and his fingertips bit deeply into her soft flesh. "You're a stupid, empty-headed slut. Not good enough to be a mother or to share my name. Worthless, except in bed." He jerked her to her feet. "And we're going to find out right now if there's been any improvement since you've been sleeping with Damas Silva."

She thought her legs wouldn't hold her as he shoved her forward. She had known that there would be a price to pay. A husband like Santini would want to humiliate his unfaithful wife in every degrading way he could. In fact, she had calculated that he would drag her off to the bedroom.

The keys to the basement files. That's all she needed. Somehow she had to get them. There seemed to be only one way.

She pretended to sob and she leaned heavily against him as they went up the stairs. He upbraided her with filthy accusations. Every word stripped her of any pride. A physical beating would not have been any more devastating, thought Alexa. How had her sister maintained any self-worth under such emotional abuse?

When they had almost reached the top step, Alexa pretended to stumble. She went down on one knee.

"Damn you...get up!" Santini swore, and reached over to pull her to her feet.

She came up swiftly. In one fierce motion, she pushed him with both hands and leaned into him with her body. The unexpected force shoved him completely off balance. Once his bulky frame was off balance he couldn't regain it.

His thick eyebrows raised in utter surprise as he fell backward. He let out a bull's roar. His heavy body tumbled head over heels, hitting harshly on every step and landing at the bottom of the stairs with a loud thud that seemed to shake the wooden floor from its foundation.

She followed him down, knelt by his still form and frantically searched his pockets. When her trembling fingers touched the key ring, she quickly took it out and had time enough to close her fingers over the keys before a rush of footsteps came pounding from the interior of the house.

"My husband...he fell," Alexa wailed in mock hysteria.

The gaunt little woman and two men hurried to Santini's side. One of the men felt for a pulse in Leo's thick throat.

"Is he...is he?" Alexa sobbed.

"He's still alive. Call a doctor." he told the woman servant.

"Better leave him where he is. I'll get a blanket," said one of the men, and bounded up the stairs.

While a whirl of activity centered everyone's attention on Santini, Alexa retreated to the living room. So far, everything was going as planned. She'd get the records from the basement room. Then, as Santini's wife, she'd insist on accompanying him either to the hospital or the morgue. As soon as she could she'd put the incriminating evidence into someone's hand.

Double adjoining doors led into a library and then out into a back hall. She slipped through the house and made her way quickly to the basement door, relieved to find it unlocked. With Leo's keys clutched in her sweaty hand, she stood in pitch-black darkness on the top landing until she located a light switch.

The dank basement was just as it had been earlier, only this time no light came from behind the old cupboard. She would have never known that there was a secret room just beyond if she hadn't seen it with her own eyes.

She could still hear footsteps pounding overhead. How long before someone discovered she was not where she should be? Had Leo left orders to clean out the incriminating files if anything went wrong? Someone could rush down to the basement at any moment. The knowledge did nothing to steady her hands as she searched for some kind of a lever or button that would swing back the cupboard. She lost precious minutes examining the wall around the cupboard. Nothing. With methodical concentration, she ran her hand over every shelf. She was about to despair, when she reached the top board and her fingers touched metal. A box like a garage door opener had been fastened to the end of the top board. She pushed it, stepped to one side as the cupboard swung outward.

A small night-light shone like a miniature beacon in the depths of the room. Just inside the opening, her fingers touched a light switch. The room blazed into light, just the way it had been before. A line of filing cabinets stood against one wall. Two computers flanked a wide office desk covered with papers, books and wire baskets.

Alexa went straight to the cabinets. All the drawers were unlocked. She swung around to the desk. There were three drawers on each side. Only a small one on the bottom had a tiny brass keyhole. Alexa searched the key ring for the smallest key and shoved it into the lock. With trembling fingers she turned it and heard a faint click. The drawer was filled with disks, ledgers and carefully sealed folders.

She was on her knees reaching into the drawer, when she felt a movement of air. Very slowly she raised her head.

''Looking for something?''

Malchek stood in the doorway, with a black revolver pointed at her head.

Chapter Twenty

Alexa got carefully to her feet as Malchek's glare of black hatred swept over her.

His lips never moved, but his eyes delivered the words. *I'm going to kill you.*

"No, wait! You don't understand," she gasped in desperation. "I...I was getting something...for Leo," she stammered. "He told me... if he was hurt or anything. My husband wanted—"

"He ain't your husband." His vicious eyes stripped her bare and his thick lips twisted. "You ain't nothing but a fake."

She opened her mouth to protest, but no words would come out. It was over. Malchek had found out. He knew it wasn't his boss's wife he was going to kill. Nothing she could say would change anything. Alexa Widmire was expendable.

"The boys just called in. Went to that apartment. Guess what they found? Photos of a blasted look-alike. A dead ringer for the boss's wife. The minute I heard it, I knew what was up! Something about you smelled from the very beginning." He gave a jerk of his thick head. "Get moving. We're going to take a walk. Even one Mia Santini is too damn much."

He clamped a bear-claw hand on one of her wrists and dragged her through the basement and up the stairs. No one was in the kitchen as he shoved her out the back door, twisting her arm painfully behind her.

The squeal of car brakes at the front of the house alerted her that the doctor and ambulance must have arrived. She got out a half scream before he clamped his free hand over her mouth and his thick fingers squeezed her nose and lips so hard that she couldn't get any air.

She twisted. Writhed. He tightened his grip. A horrible sensation of suffocating enveloped her. Devoid of air, her lungs burned. Her head began to balloon with sudden lightness.

Malchek dragged her across the ground, behind the outbuildings and into a thick drift of trees.

"You shouldn't have hurt the boss," he growled. "Now I got to kill you quick. Not take my time about it the way I like to do." There was a chilling regret in his voice.

Alexa had nearly passed out from lack of air when he threw her down into a dense undergrowth of shrubs and trees. He looked like the devil himself standing over her. With a twist of his lips that passed for a smile, he pointed the gun at her heart.

THE SHERIFF'S CAR was right behind the ambulance when it stopped in front of the house, and a second official vehicle filled with four deputies pulled in at the same time. Damas was the first one out of the sheriff's car. He was almost to the front steps, when he heard a distant muffled cry that sounded like an animal in pain. He listened again. Nothing.

He bounded through the front door on the ambulance attendants' heels. Leo Santini was stretched out on the floor at the bottom of the stairs. His labored breathing sounded like a leaking air hose. Someone had put a pillow under his head and blanket over him. Only the distraught little woman hovered at his side, blubbering about a fall.

Out of the corner of his eyes. Damas saw two men dart out down the hall and race for the back door. They'd just gotten outside, when they ran straight into two deputies who had circled the house.

"Where is she?" Damas grabbed one of the fleeing men by the throat. "Tell me or I'll snap your neck like a chicken's."

The man threw his eyes and head toward the wooded area beyond the outbuildings. "Malchek…" he sputtered. "Malchek took her."

Damas raced across the ground. His thudding footsteps sounded loudly as he left the clearing and bolted into the thick wood. Standing over Alexa, Malchek spun around. Someone was moving fast through the trees. Then, as suddenly as the loud movement had begun, it stopped.

"What the hell…" swore Malchek. He pointed his revolver in the direction of the now-silent footsteps. "Show yourself or die," he yelled.

Silence. Then Malchek fired.

Damas clamped down on his breath. He pressed up against a green lichened tree trunk and slipped his .38 from his holster. Malchek's voice and the shot had come from the left, beyond a drift of thick trees and undergrowth.

A moment later, Damas glimpsed a black shadow moving through the trees. Menacing. Threatening. Alexa? Where was she? Was he holding her in front of him as a shield?

Had Malchek already killed her?

Damas crouched low, waiting. Layered shadows blended light and dark, making a single tree, rock or man indistinct. The only sound in the deathly stillness was the flutter of birds overhead as they took off. Damas cursed under his breath. The frightened birds could signal his position.

Damas took a cautious step forward. Another shot rang out and clipped a limb just above his head, raining shattered leaves and splintered wood down upon him. He ducked down, scurried into a depression where young fir trees were reaching for the sun.

The flash of Malchek's gun had told Damas that the chauffeur was stealthily moving closer and closer toward him. Damas wanted to fire back some random shots at him, but he didn't dare until he knew where Alexa was.

Hunched over, Damas moved quickly along the ditchlike depression. The natural hollow gave him some concealment for a short distance until the ground began to rise again. When the hollow ended, he left the stand of fir trees. If he had calculated right. He was now in a position to play Malchek's own game by coming up behind him.

He had calculated wrong. Malchek had turned back!

As Damas moved forward, some tall wild bushes suddenly parted. There was Malchek. Both men froze. Face-to-face only a few yards apart like opponents in a duel, they aimed raised guns at each other.

"Where is she, you bastard?" Damas demanded.

Malchek smiled and fired.

Searing fire stabbed Damas's left arm, but the .38 in his other hand remained steady. His aim was true. Malchek's heavy body fell to the ground. His beady gray eyes were wide open as Damas stepped over his body and raced through the trees, one arm dangling at his side.

When he saw Alexa lying lifeless on the ground, he flung himself down beside her and cradled her in his one good arm. Her eyes flickered upward, bewildered at first, and then softening as she took in his dirty, sweaty face.

"Thank God," he breathed.

She gave him a wan smile. "What took you so long?"

Chapter Twenty-One

They walked along the beach, breathing the salty air of Bar Harbor. Graceful sailboats dotted the gently rolling waters, and on the horizon the ocean and sky melded in a luminous glow.

One of Damas's arms was in a sling and he had the other around Alexa's waist. They walked in rhythm, their legs brushing in teasing intimacy as their bare feet sank deeply into the soft sand. Behind them Mia sat on a blanket with Dorrie, and they could hear her laughing as she played with the baby.

Alexa exchanged a smile with Damas. "What's the old saying? 'All's well that ends well'?"

"Something like that. Does your sister know how lucky she is?"

"I'm the lucky one," countered Alexa. "No more empty holidays. No more loneliness filling up my boring life. Both Mia and Dorrie are going to need me. My sister's already filed for divorce. She'll face some big changes in her life."

"She's lucky to get a second chance. When Leo gets out of the hospital he'll stand trial, and with the evidence against him, he'll probably spend the rest of his life behind bars." Damas chuckled. "I can't believe that I came out of this with a promotion. When your impersonation resulted in Leo kidnapping someone who wasn't his wife, Captain Talbot had to change his tune. He's taking credit for the indictment, of course."

"He ought to thank Jack Powers."

Damas nodded. "He's the one who pulled the fat out of the fire, all right."

"Everything seems to have been settled satisfactorily," she said tentatively, without looking at him.

He stopped, pulled her close and held her firmly against him with his one good arm. "Really? I was thinking there are a couple of loose ends. What do you think? I've got a little recuperation time coming and you have two more weeks before classes start. We ought to be able to find something to do besides running and hiding, getting shot and kidnapped."

"It wasn't all bad," she insisted. "I miss having the baby and... being a family."

He laughed and tipped her chin. "I know how we might remedy the situation."

From the way she slipped her arms around his neck, he knew what her answer would be when he asked the lady a very important question.

HARLEQUIN®

Deceit, betrayal, murder

Join Harlequin's intrepid heroines, India Leigh
and Mary Hadfield, as they ferret out the truth
behind the mysterious goings-on in their
neighborhood. These two women are no milk-
and-water misses. In fact, they thrive on

MISCHIEF & MAYHEM

Watch for their incredible adventures in this
special two-book collection. Available in March,
wherever Harlequin books are sold.

HARLEQUIN®

I N T R I G U E®

Into a world where danger lurks around
every corner, and there's a fine line between trust
and betrayal, comes a tall, dark and handsome man.

Intuition draws you to him...but instinct keeps you
away. Is he really one of those...

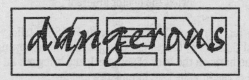

Don't miss even one of the twelve sexy but secretive
men, coming to you one per month in 1995.

In March, look for
#313 A KILLER SMILE
by Laura Kenner

**Take a walk on the wild side...with our
"DANGEROUS MEN"!**

Available wherever Harlequin books are sold.

DM-2

HARLEQUIN®

I N T R I G U E®

Brush up on your bedside manner with...

Three heart-racing romantic-suspense novels that are just
what the doctor ordered!

This spring, Harlequin Intrigue presents PULSE, a trilogy of
medical thrillers by Carly Bishop to get your blood flowing,
raise the hairs on the back of your neck and bring out all the
telltale of reading the best in romance and mystery.

Don't miss your appointments with:

#314 HOT BLOODED
March 1995

#319 BREATHLESS
April 1995

#323 HEART THROB
May 1995

What if...

You'd agreed to marry a man you'd never met, in a town where you'd never been, while surrounded by wedding guests you'd never seen before?

And what if...

You weren't sure you could trust the man to whom you'd given your hand?

Look for "Mail Order Brides"—the upcoming two novels of romantic suspense by Cassie Miles, which are available in April and July—and only from Harlequin Intrigue!

Don't miss

> #320 MYSTERIOUS VOWS
> by Cassie Miles
> April 1995

Mail Order Brides—where mail-order marriages lead distrustful newlyweds into the mystery and romance of a lifetime!

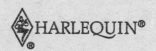

Harlequin invites you to the most
romantic wedding of the season.

Rope the cowboy of your dreams in
Marry Me, Cowboy!

A collection of 4 brand-new stories,
celebrating weddings, written by:

New York Times bestselling author

JANET DAILEY

and favorite authors

Margaret Way
Anne McAllister
Susan Fox

Be sure not to miss Marry Me, Cowboy!
coming this April

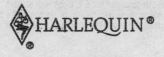
HARLEQUIN®

MMC

HARLEQUIN®

Don't miss these Harlequin favorites by some of our most distinguished authors!
And now, you can receive a discount by ordering two or more titles!

HT#25577	WILD LIKE THE WIND by Janice Kaiser	$2.99	☐
HT#25589	THE RETURN OF CAINE O'HALLORAN by JoAnn Ross	$2.99	☐
HP#11626	THE SEDUCTION STAKES by Lindsay Armstrong	$2.99	☐
HP#11647	GIVE A MAN A BAD NAME by Roberta Leigh	$2.99	☐
HR#03293	THE MAN WHO CAME FOR CHRISTMAS by Bethany Campbell	$2.89	☐
HR#03308	RELATIVE VALUES by Jessica Steele	$2.89	☐
SR#70589	CANDY KISSES by Muriel Jensen	$3.50	☐
SR#70598	WEDDING INVITATION by Marisa Carroll	$3.50 U.S. $3.99 CAN.	☐
HI#22230	CACHE POOR by Margaret St. George	$2.99	☐
HAR#16515	NO ROOM AT THE INN by Linda Randall Wisdom	$3.50	☐
HAR#16520	THE ADVENTURESS by M.J. Rodgers	$3.50	☐
HS#28795	PIECES OF SKY by Marianne Willman	$3.99	☐
HS#28824	A WARRIOR'S WAY by Margaret Moore	$3.99 U.S. $4.50 CAN.	☐

(limited quantities available on certain titles)

	AMOUNT	$
DEDUCT:	**10% DISCOUNT FOR 2+ BOOKS**	$
ADD:	**POSTAGE & HANDLING**	$
	($1.00 for one book, 50¢ for each additional)	
	APPLICABLE TAXES*	$_____
	TOTAL PAYABLE	$_____
	(check or money order—please do not send cash)	

To order, complete this form and send it, along with a check or money order for the total above, payable to Harlequin Books, to: **In the U.S.:** 3010 Walden Avenue, P.O. Box 9047, Buffalo, NY 14269-9047; **In Canada:** P.O. Box 613, Fort Erie, Ontario, L2A 5X3.

Name: _____

Address: _____ City: _____

State/Prov.: _____ Zip/Postal Code: _____

*New York residents remit applicable sales taxes.
  Canadian residents remit applicable GST and provincial taxes.

HBACK-JM2